Beside the Seaside and Other Tales

all the
best,
from

Roy Kenridge

TRADE   MARK

Beside the Seaside
&
Other Tales

*

ROY KERRIDGE

SWANSEA
The Brynmill Publishing Company
1974

The Brynmill Publishing Company Limited
130, Bryn Road, Brynmill, Swansea SA2 0AT

first published 1974

all rights reserved

ISBN 0 9502723 2 9

printed by
The John Penry Press
11 St. Helen's Road, Swansea

CONTENTS

Beside the Seaside   *page* 9

The Story of David   73

The Painter and the Church   173

These stories are all dedicated to my sister Joma
—Queen of Nannies.

Beside the Seaside

If you can't do the bird, don't do the crime.

Old Brighton Proverb

For my best friend—B E R Y L

" Funny feeling, isn't it, the first time you carve a bloke's face up? "

" You're right there. My first time, I felt quite sick, but you can get used to anything. "

This interesting conversation took place below the ground, not in Hades, but in Brighton, that popular holiday resort. It could have been overheard by anyone who had taken the trouble to bend an ear over the grating that covered the tiny window of the basement of a betting shop, on that cold out-of-season day in the middle 'sixties. The betting shop itself was a gloomy building in a gloomy little lane that connected the shopping centre to the seafront. At the end of the lane, the sea stood like an erect grey wall, filling the air with a wintry spray as one approached. One side of the street was partially taken up by a once-popular variety theatre, now a Bingo Hall. This recent metamorphosis accounted, along with the weather, for the lane's damply despondent character, for most of the buildings were theatrical boarding houses whose owners now faced certain ruin. Yet the houses were not without charm, for their roofs were tiled haphazardly in blue-grey slate, and their hindquarters, wreathed in drain pipes and curly iron fire escapes, were built of Sussex flint in the same pattern as a stone wall in the countryside. Adjoining the Bingo Hall stood a large empty hotel, whose many curiously shaped windows were boarded up or draped in coils of barbed wire. Along its tiled roof, attic windows stood in ill-assorted rows, each attic being as if a tiny house in its own right, with a pinnacled roof that gave the impression of a witch's cottage. Some of these attics were still inhabited by the few remaining staff members, who now ran a social club in what was once the dining hall.

Across the road was the betting shop, a rival to the hotel, and in the billiards room downstairs, our two conversationalists were holding forth.

The first was a stout red-faced young man, with sleepy eyes, broken teeth, and a smiling expression of arrogance and low cunning. His black, greasy hair flopped over his forehead, and when he spoke, even as now to his best friend and elder brother, he seemed to shout defiantly.

The second of the two Coker Brothers, scourge of the South Coast, was a far more striking character. Tall and well built, he resembled his youthful idol, the film star Tony Curtis. One of his lean, sunken cheeks was slashed across the bone by a streak of long-healed red and white, which suggested correctly that he could take a carving-up as stoically as he could dish one out. But it was in Frank Coker's eyes that could be seen the quality of success that made him stand above the run-of-the-mill hooliganism of his brother Ozzie. Frank had no need of Ozzie's device of slit-eyed amusedly bored menace. His own eyes, which were large, brown, and yet with a steely glitter, gazed straight into those of any stranger or slight acquaintance he might meet. If Frank smiled and made one of his little jokes, the stranger would laugh uneasily and later, flattered and relieved, dine out on the episode for weeks. Whereas, if Frank looked serious, the stranger would shake, stammer and commend his soul to God. Notwithstanding his hobby of collecting unusual pistols and practicing marksmanship, Frank had never killed anyone, as he considered

murder to be both dangerous and childish. No, if he had
to, he would use a knife, or more usually a forehead and
a boot, but generally he found that one of his quietly
sardonic talks would do the trick. Ozzie was far less
subtle, and fought for pleasure, sometimes even using
a small axe. Both were well-known figures around the
clubs and late-night cafés, where they were treated as
kings and given anything they wanted. Frank also
mixed in the relatively polite society of hearty young
sports-car owners in sheepskin jackets, who joked with
him familiarly and considered him a businessman of sorts,
only half-believing the rumours of his criminal career.
Unknown to his brother, Frank had outgrown the
idealism of his early Teddy Boy days, and planned to
use villainy as a mere stepping stone to legitimate
success, instead of as an end in itself.

Needless to say, both Coker brothers were always
dressed, as on this occasion, in the very smartest suits,
white shirts and slim ties. No slag they, but the essence
of sophistication, Brighton-style. The tiny room they
were in contained a television on a shelf, a billiard table
and a beefy young man in a belted mackintosh, asleep
on a chair. If service of any kind was wanted, the young
man could be awoken by switching off the television,
the resulting silence being enough to send him springing
to his feet. However, the Cokers saw no need to disturb
him after a hard night stealing lead, and wiping the
chalk plans they had made, military fashion, for a robbery
in Hastings, from the green baize, they departed for the
more convivial atmosphere of the social club across the
road.

At the top of the stairs, they edged respectfully around

the pram that stood across the open doorway. Ozzie stood grinning impatiently while Frank gazed at the proprietor's tiny baby with grim sentimentality.

"Poor little bleeder," said Frank. "Little does 'e know what 'e's letting 'imself in for."

"Yeh, poor little perisher," agreed Ozzie, laughing oafishly and swinging into his jaunty "get off the pavement, you" stride, as he led the way. Both Cokers took it for granted that the child would grow up into a world of violence, robbery, terror and prison sentences. Dismissing its fate from their minds, they pushed aside a rusty iron gate and entered, by way of a mouldering arched doorway, the cobbled, rubbish-strewn mews of the decaying hotel. Stepping around the puddles, and avoiding the water that dripped from a crazy conglomeration of drainpipes, they reached the old kitchen door, walked along a narrow staff corridor, and finally reached their destination.

This was a vast, brightly lit hall, where genial loafers from every walk of life played cards or snooker. As the Cokers strode inside, conversation didn't quite stop, but it seemed to flicker uneasily and then continue. The Cokers swaggered past the card tables, loudly cracking jokes to each other. At the snooker tables they paused to favour some sharp young players with a word or two. Every table was occupied, many of them by Persian so-called students, who swore prodigiously and then laughed at their own wit.

"More Persians than people, these days," observed Frank.

"We're just finishing this game," said an English youth, ingratiatingly.

" No hurry, old son," Frank answered kindly.

A middle-aged man in a baggy grey suit, who had been buying a cup of tea from the hatch in the wall, spun around and stared at the elder Coker.

" Well, bless my soul, Gawd help us, look who it isn't, if it's not Frank Coker, well, well, well! " said this person, putting his cup down on a table and shaking Frank's hand with enthusiasm.

Frank watched his hand being shaken with interest, and then gazed hard at his new companion's drink-flushed face.

" Wandsworth Reception, nineteen sixty three! " he exclaimed. Ozzie looked on keenly.

" That's it, the old firm, the old firm! " shouted the man cheerfully. He was unabashed heartiness itself, fat, bald, boozy and red-nosed, yet as gleeful and boyish as a youth on his first pub-crawl. Something in his manner appealed to Frank's long-buried softer side. Recently, Frank had been reflecting that a sinister reputation was something of a cross to bear. Now he would unbend a little.

" What was it you got done for? " he enquired mildly.

" A trifling matter of embezzlement. Never again, my old squire, never again! The food was not at all what I've been accustomed to, nor the discipline for that matter. And I've been in some funny places—public school, the Army, the military nick and the coal mines for the duration of the war. What were you doing in there? "

" I came, I broke, I entered! " announced Frank histrionically, getting into the feel of things. " Crime doesn't pay, but the hours are good," Ozzie chimed in. This was his favourite joke, and he guffawed mightily.

" You been in civvy street long? " pursued Frank.

" Salesman, aren't I? Juke boxes is my line. Been with the same firm for two years since I was de-nickified, and now the governor's sent me down here to drum up trade. Got to sink or swim, you know. Family's disowned me. Now, care for a game of rummy? "

An hour later, they were all firm friends. The salesman's name was Maurice, and he especially intrigued Frank by his curious mixture of Cockney brashness and upper-class languor. Ozzie took all his leads from Frank, and if Frank thought this nutcase was all right, then all right he must be. Maurice himself remembered Frank as the big-hearted gent who could butter up the screws and provide snout for all, in return for various small favours. Vaguely, he remembered tales and rumours of Frank beating up and kicking those who did not co-operate, but he dismissed these from his good-natured mind. Soon, in the social and anti-social clubs of Brighton, Frank, Ozzie and Maurice became known as the Three Musketeers.

Weeks passed, and then months. Ozzie found their passing tedious, for having been apprehended in unlawful possession of a juke box, he had been sentenced to nine months by the judge at the Lewes Sessions. Maurice, who was also implicated, was acquitted thanks to lack of evidence, but he lost his job. Frank had been enjoying a love affair with an au-pair girl, and had not involved himself at all. Somehow he procured for Maurice a wad of carefully prepared references, and the latter took a well-paid job as a caller in the Bingo Hall.

So, while Ozzie was mouldering as a Stores Orderly, Maurice moved into his brother's smart flat on Hove seafront, and took over his niche. Coached by Frank, he assisted in the robbery of silver, jewellery and antiques from the home of the au-pair girl's employers. Fortune, that fickle goddess, smiled on Maurice and Frank that winter. The au-pair girl, tired of Frank referring to her as his "slave", returned to Sweden to train as a probation officer. In the Hove flat, life became a merry round of parties and gaiety.

Frank Coker, at this time, was a highly successful and respected member of his profession. Roguery, however, has its amateurs as well as its professionals. One of these amateurs was Dave Prentice, aptly named, for though a mere beginner in the art of villainy, fortune was to raise him briefly to Coker-type heights.

Dave sat in his bedsitting room in Oriental Place, on one freezing February evening, feeling intensely self-pitying. He was a tall young man in his late twenties, and though clean, short-haired and respectably dressed, in casual clothes as worn by clerks, he looked undeniably seedy. This may have been due to his strong feeling of being an underdog. Everything was the fault of They, whoever They might be. How could a poor working man survive, Dave reasoned to himself, when he was ground underfoot by either the Royal Family, the Old Boy Network, the Government, the Capitalists or the Ruling Classes (Dave wasn't sure which)? A look of pure, monkey-like malice crept into his usually frank and childish features. The trouble was that They had forced him, by remote control, into a betting shop, where he had lost most of his poor workingman's dole money. From They it had come, and to They it had returned.

Moodily, he huddled in front of his flaring gas fire. When winter comes to bedsitterland, the gas fire becomes the centre of everything, the jealous God to whom precious shilling pieces must be sacrificed. Dave and his fire seemed to carry on a love-hate relationship. Should he crouch too near the flames he would be burned, but if he pulled his chair back even a couple of inches he would freeze, for the heat went straight up the chimney. What made the situation so bitterly ironical was that Dave knew perfectly well how to rob and rig the meter, but as he was on probation for this very misdeed in a previous lodging, he dare not try it again. Nor could he put a shilling in, as all that remained of his dole was the two pounds needed to pay the rent. Dave gave a scornful laugh at his beloved tormentor, the fire. The fire responded by going out, and Dave swore at the top of his voice. As if in mockery, the jets of flame, now each a mere heatless half inch in height, wobbled back at him. Angrily, Dave turned the switch, and the fire gave a bang and was extinct. What was so maddening was that the fire went out with the same bang when nearly dead, as now, as when in roaring life.

Nostalgically Dave cast his mind back to far-off November, when his fire was always blazing. This was because the Labour Exchange had, at great expense, brought in a computer which took a liking to Dave, or so it seemed. For this amiable machine had paid him three amounts of dole a week, at fifteen pounds a time, for the duration of the month. By December the affairs of the Labour Exchange were in such confusion that four new clerks had to be employed to do the work of the computer. The computer itself was kept on as a prestige-worthy pet. Dave was summoned to the Labour Exchange by a sternly worded note, and he came in fear and trembling. He was then, to his amazement and relief, awarded a seventeen pound rebate, as a last farewell gesture from the computer. Dave was, of course, unable to work because of his "nervous trouble". The thought of work always made him nervous, though in his time he had been an embezzling bus conductor, an embezzling deck-chair attendant and, strange to say, an embezzling ice-cream salesman. Each time They had caused him to be dismissed from his chosen profession. In the summer, he drew his dole and also washed cars, cleaned windows and sometimes did a little beach photography—tourists by day and drunk sailors by night. Now it was too cold to work, naturally. His camera was in pawn, and he spent half his time in bed and half in pubs, where he stole lighters and other odds and ends whenever possible. Obviously he was meant to be a great man, but They, fearful of his competition, were determined to keep him down.

Groaning, he climbed the stairs to his friend's room, hoping to borrow a shilling. He detested his friend, as he had had to sell him his only overcoat some weeks ago. Nevertheless, they had boasted of thieving so much to one another as to create a mutual bond of distrust.

"You there, Bob?" he asked, banging on the door. Bob let him in good-humouredly. He was a short thick-set young migrant labourer from the Midlands, with a smiling, quietly spoken manner, yet with something rather secretive about him. Dave had sat down on the one rickety wooden chair before he noticed a third party was present, in the shape of a slim young man with tousled greasy hair, who was kneeling down trying to break the gas meter off the wall, partly by unscrewing it and partly by hitting it with a boot.

" Evenin', mate, " Dave said politely.

" Evenin', " acknowledged the youth, looking up for a brief moment and then returning absorbedly to the work in hand.

Bob chatted away about his job for a while, but noticing that Dave seemed uneasy, explained that he had dented the lock on his door, so that if there were any repercussions, he could say his room had been broken into by a person or persons unknown.

" I'm always short of spendin' money by the middle of the week, " he added.

" I'm always short of spendin' money, full stop, " Dave answered with one of his bitter laughs.

" Well, why don't you get a job? "

" You'll never get me co-operating with the System, " was the dark reply. " It's bad enough having to sign on at the Labour, what with all that queuing before I get my money. Better be on the dole than be dependent on the System. "

" Only System I know owt about is the one I used at the dog track, and that went for a burton, " rejoined his companion, to whose obscure corner of Staffordshire the latest intellectual ideas had not yet penetrated.

Their discourse was suddenly interrupted by a loud crash, a rip of wall-paper and a sound of falling plaster. Proudly, Bob's friend laid a severed chunk of gas meter on the bed, and they all gazed at it with the awed silence due to a fallen idol.

" Thing is, " said the young man, " to break open the cash box from the rear. Then I can fix it back on the wall, like, and the padlock'll still be all okay. Need to force it, like."

Intrigued, they gathered around and poked and levered at the cold, grey recumbent gas meter. Finally, Bob, having broken a screwdriver, a fork and a pair of scissors, seized the chair and with a mighty effort broke off one of its legs. He fitted the splintered end into a cavity, gave the other end a jerk, and bang! the job was done. With a loud report, the meter flew open and showered six shillings around the room. Dave tried to sneak one for himself, but as if anticipating this, Bob was down on his knees in a flash and soon gathered up the loot.

"That's all right—enough for three halves down the pub," he announced complacently, "I'll fix the meter back on Friday, when I can get a new screwdriver. Shouldn't cost me more than a few bob." Feeling very jaunty and cheerful, the three conspirators sauntered out into the wide world. Dave greatly enjoyed the warm togetherness of criminality, a world of excitement, danger and romance. Today, spectator of a gas meter robbery, tomorrow the Royal Mail. The pub was bleak and neon lit, with rubber seats, but the bombast of the ruffianly crowd partly compensated for this. As in most Southern cities, the new enlightenment had caused the younger native workmen to grow ashamed of their labour and to consider the "spike", or dole, to be a more honourable source of income until such time as they could be magically raised to their true station in life. To fill the gap, labourers from the North, from Ireland and from Scotland had settled in to do the work, and the pub catered especially for these newcomers. The young men wore suits and fought, and the older men wore baggy grey clothes and got drunk. Apart from a few hard-faced prostitutes, the only women present were aged and slatternly. Something interesting always happened here, thought Dave, who remembered the time when an old man had repeatedly cut his wrists with glasses he had broken for the purpose, despite being continually prevented by nearby well-wishers. Eventually, the police had dragged him out into an ambulance, but even as he was dragged, he cut himself again.

Blood was all over the pavement, and a gang of youths had turned up to gaze at it, pushing each other and roaring with laughter. Dave had lived on the excitement for weeks.

However, when they had downed their murky, watery bitter, Bob rose as if to go home, and his friend too. This was far too anti-climactic an ending to such a brilliant evening, and Dave, still feeling devil-may-care, decided to stay on, and squander his rent money after all. What was life, he felt, without romance? Romance in this establishment was supplied by either Boney Maronie or Dirty Maureen, neither of them very prepossessing. As Dave had once caught a fell disease from Boney Maronie, he decided on Maureen, who was an unknown quantity. Looking into her cheap, snaggle-toothed features, he thought he divined a glimpse of something tender, loving and passionate. Maureen's eyes met his, and looked enquiring. Dave nodded, and the girl walked outside. Playing for time, Dave drank long and deeply from his empty glass, and then caught her up.

" Long time or short time? " she asked.

" Long time, " he replied, and they walked on without speaking. As often, Dirty Maureen swore savagely to herself, under her breath, calling down curses upon the world until they reached their destination. This was a basement flat with access to bedrooms upstairs.

Maureen thumped on the door, uttered an oath, and they were admitted by the caretaker. Despite the time of year, this person wore a string vest, beneath which his stomach bulged outwards and hung over his tightened belt. Bar a few wisps, the caretaker's head was bald, but his hairy arms and doormat chest amply made up for this. He was blind in one eye, and as he greeted them, he yawned and scratched his glass eye absently.

" I'll tell Michael, " he said, leaving them in the kitchen. The door of the front room was open, and Dave wistfully glimpsed a group of ponces, young and old, drinking beer from bottles that were passed around, and joking cheerfully amongst themselves. Dave felt he had missed his vocation. It looked so cosy in there, especially now that a raddle-faced Scottish girl was dancing, brandishing a cider bottle and singing "The Northern Lights of Old Aberdeen".

" Mine, is it? " said a voice, and Michael appeared, a nasty looking young Irishman, with an ape-like forehead, small beady eyes and dark slicked-back hair.

" Long time, " Maureen reported.

" Two pounds, " said Michael, holding out his hand rather curtly. Dave paid, and followed Maureen up the stairs, shivering with fear and anticipation. Michael, he felt, had committed a breach of etiquette, as he had spoiled the make-believe of a genuine romance and a kindly parting gift, given unasked-for. Normally

Michael avoided Maureen's friends and carried on the make-believe himself, but they had had a quarrel over money. "Ponce" and "prostitute" were very dirty words in that establishment.

In the bedroom, Maureen quickly disrobed and then opened a Pepsi Cola bottle. With one hand she held the bottle to her mouth, and with the other she beckoned to Dave to get ready. She put down the bottle, dealt swiftly with Dave, and then finished it before the fizz ran out.

Slowly, Dave pulled up his trousers, feeling terribly cheated. Two pounds for one moment of brief excitement! A whole week's rent money thrown away—it was scandalous! Briskly, Maureen prepared to visit the pub once more before closing time. Dave looked at her in agony. Where was the rapture, the ecstasy, the Paradise for which he had yearned? As Maureen picked up her handbag and made for the door, Dave found his tongue at last.

"That was never a long time!" he shouted. "Short time, that was!"

"That was a long time!"

"Short time!"

"Long time! Now get bleedin' lost or I'll 'ave to fetch Michael."

"I'll see your bleedin' Michael myself!" cried Dave rashly. Now fully dressed, he ran into the front room, closely followed by Maureen.

In their absence, the cordial atmosphere had been spoilt by the sudden flare-up of yet another quarrel. One ponce had called another ponce a ponce, and naturally there would now be murders.

"I'm not a ponce, I'm a gipsy!" retorted the ponce

of the second part proudly, rising to his full height. At that moment, Dave burst in hysterically, and accosted Michael.

" I want my pound back! I paid for long time, and I got short time! "

" 'E never! " shrilled Maureen, falling through the doorway. " 'E paid for long time an' I give 'im long time! 'Ow long does 'e think long time is, anyway? "

" It's longer'n short time, which is what you give me! "

" Long time! "

" Short time! "

" This is an outrage! " shouted the caretaker, and he thereupon punched Dave on the chest and sent him sprawling.

Michael, the gipsy, and the other ponce, their rift healed, sprang to where Dave lay. But the thoughtful caretaker restrained them.

" Don't kick 'is head in here, boys, " he appealed. " Mess up the carpet an' smash up the furniture, it will. Take him out the back yard an' do 'im over, then you can chuck 'im out in the back alley when you're done. "

As if in a nightmare, Dave felt himself lifted by an arm and two legs, and hoisted along the corridor. Maureen, who hated all men, smiled delightedly and then went back to the pub to find someone else. In the cold, gritty yard, Dave hit the ground, but before the onslaught of steel-tipped heels could begin, a commanding voice from the darkness ordered them to stop it.

It was Frank Coker, immaculate as ever, and making a discreet entrance by the back way in order to collect protection money—a small side-line of his. Everyone stood and looked at him, and Dave, amazed to find himself still in one piece, crawled over and stood up too.

" 'E was being awkward, " explained the gipsy.

" If anyone's crunched around here, it's me who does the crunching, " Frank explained. " You'll get closed down if you carry on like this. Where are you going? " he suddenly shouted, catching Dave by the tie as the latter attempted a pathetic tip-toe to freedom.

" Er—er, " said Dave.

" Don't get funny with me, " Frank ordered. " What's 'e done, anyway? " No one answered. Such was Frank's power, that they stood shamefaced.

" I paid for long time and the girl give me short time, " Dave faltered eventually, in a small piping voice that he hardly recognised.

"My godfathers!" said Frank sarcastically. "I thought you'd at least killed someone. Well, hoppit, get lost: there's a gate over there, so use it. I can't waste my time standing here forever. "

" Thank you sir! " Dave babbled, and off he flew. Outside, he stood shaking, propped against a wall, for some minutes. He hoarsely talked to himself, and eventually reassured, he hurried back towards his digs, wondering what to tell his landlady next day.

As he passed a smart and prosperous public house, he paused to think enviously of They, in Their neat suits, who were carousing within, squandering money that rightfully was his. A hard clip-clop of footsteps arrested his attention, as did a familiar voice, which asked him if drinks were still being served.

Looking up, he saw, to his horror, the kind stranger who had stayed the boots of his persecutors.

" Gawd strewth, it's you again, Nimrod! " said
Frank, his good humour belying his dangerous glint.
" I suppose you're skint. Come in an' have a drink. "

Dumbfoundedly, Dave followed this Angel of Mercy.
Inside, a new world was revealed to Dave, who himself
was an unhappy child of that unhappy experiment,
Crawley New Town. Gracious living was a new
experience for him, and he looked wonderingly at the
oak panels, the wooden beams, the ornate lampshades
and the rows of hanging pewter mugs. A thick carpet
was beneath his feet and, not far from a blazing coal fire,
a polished table groaned beneath the weight of piles of
magazines—*Punch*, *Queen* and the *Daily Telegraph* colour
supplement.

Frank nodded good evening to several nodding
acquaintances—a benevolent ex-colonel with a white
moustache, a bleary eyed woman in a tweed coat
and some elderly businessmen—while Dave trailed
awkwardly behind, smiling feebly. They were just in
time to be served, and Frank's generosity could be
explained by the fact that the young barman gave him
drinks on the house.

" You must be very popular here, " Dave ventured
nervously.

" It's not that. The bloke here owes me something.
He took my girl out, years ago, in 'is motor, behind my
back. They 'ad a smash-up, an' he lived while she died. "

" Oh, I'm sorry. "

" Why be sorry? You drink up an' be thankful. I've
'ad free drinks off 'im ever since. "

Dave digested this in silence, while Frank and the
barman chatted, their voices lowered. Poor Dave had

only liked to ask for half a brown, and Frank was drinking lager and lime and eating ham sandwiches with lashings of mustard. Trying not to look at the ham, Dave eavesdropped on his patron's conversation. This was about a popular murder of the day, the work of a London protection mob who had been seen shooting a book-maker, but who all pleaded Not Guilty. The corpse of the bookmaker could not be found.

" You worked for them, so you know their form, " said the barman cautiously. " Tell me—is it right the body'll be in a concrete bridge foundation? "

" Chopped up an' fed to pigs, " said Frank shortly, but with a certain relish. Abruptly he greeted some hearty young men he spied in a corner, and carried his plate of ham over towards them. Absently, Dave wondered if the ham came from the same pigs who had eaten the bookmaker, and if so, would it be cannibalism to eat it, with or without mustard? His only prospect of eating next day would be if he managed to call on someone just as food was being cooked. He tried to foist his unwelcome presence on his friends on a fair rota basis, so that any one of them, having given him a meal, would be immune from a further visit for at least two weeks.

" You know Frank well, then? " asked the barman in a surprised and mildly respectful tone that interrupted Dave's meditations.

" Eh? Frank who? "

" That's Frank Coker you've just been drinking with, didn't you know? "

" Frank *Coker*? "

Dave, as he made this query, also gave a violent

start and choked over his drink. A certain amount of coughing and spluttering then took place, after which he withdrew several yards further away from Frank and began to tremble. Frank Coker, the most dreaded of the two dreaded Coker brothers! Everyone who wanted to be anyone in Brighton, in Dave's circle, had to pretend to be a friend of Frank Coker, as Dave had done himself many a time. In a strange way, he had come to look on Frank Coker as a mythical Being, whose often quoted exploits were actually as legendary as any tales of earlier Gods. Now here he was in the flesh, and treating him, Dave, to drinks, as well as saving his life.

Mentally, he began to cast and mould sentences to say to Bob.

"Had a spot of luck after you'd gone," he would say. "Ran into old Frank Coker and he bought me one. Oh yes, *the* Frank Coker, all right. We've known each other quite some time."

It seemed a pity to Dave that he should ever leave the pleasant surroundings and influential company in which he now found himself. Might not this episode be the start of a new life, of a rise to still greater glories? On another impulse, Dave ran after Frank when the latter left, and earnestly begged for the privilege of a word in the Great One's ear.

"Now what?" snapped Frank. Hadn't he done enough for this whippersnapper?

"Oh—er—I wondered if, to show my appreciation, I could be of service to you in any way. I could do odd jobs, like, in return for food, and perhaps somewhere to sleep, 'cos I can't pay rent where I am, so you see I could be of great use to you."

" That's your game, eh? I give you food an' kip, and that's the way you make yourself useful. Hmm. Are you honest and industrious? "

" Yes, yes. "

" That's no bloody use, then. Hoppit. "

However, Dave's babyish features looked so crest-fallen, almost like a scolded puppy, that Frank slightly relented. Dave appealed to his sense of the ridiculous. For one thing, the bloke's involuntary habit of excitedly hopping from one foot to another, despite his lanky frame, was comical in the extreme.

" D'you know what's meant by a tea-leaf? " Frank therefore pursued.

" Oh yes, yes. I can thieve anything you tell me to, you'll see. "

" You don't need to thieve a thing, just turn a blind eye and keep shtoom if you're to join our happy little household. If I let you move into our flat, I've got to trust you. Can I trust you? "

Dave was almost unable to believe his ears! If they did not deceive him, he was being offered the chance of membership in the Coker Gang! Overwhelmed by the honour, he gulped and then nodded eagerly. Frank gave him a charming two-faced smile and then led the way to Dave's new home, an elegant flat in a Regency house facing the angry sea.

Inside, Dave was confronted by Maurice, who looked at him just as a minor Roman official might have looked at an unsatisfactory new slave. Since his association with Frank Coker, Maurice had grown grotesquely fat. He surveyed Dave with his stomach extended and his hands in his pockets but thumbs extended outwards like pistols, while his braces stood out like tightened violin strings over his starched shirt and pot belly.

" Gor blimey, what's this you've brought me? " he demanded coarsely. " The Playboy of the Western World? "

" This is Dave, " announced Frank with what sounded like heavily veiled sarcasm. " He's going to work for us. "

" Is he? *Is* he? What does he do—snatch handbags twice daily with matinees on Wednesday and Saturday? "

" I'm game for anything, " Dave muttered doughtily.

" We've got a nice aristocratic kind of gaff here, " explained Frank in a kindly manner to Dave. " So if you're game for anything, as you say, we'll fix you up with a bed in the servant's room, and you can start work tomorrow. "

" What do I do? " asked Dave in great excitement. He didn't suppose he'd be given a gun straight away— perhaps he'd drive the getaway car, that'd be good. Similarly, he doubted if he'd be shown how to handle gelignite on so short an acquaintanceship—more likely he'd stand nick, or look-out, and that'd be hank too.

" There's an alarm-clock in the room, " Frank told him. " Set it for seven, then as soon as you've got up, you make the tea and knock on the bedroom doors. We'll get up then, and get stuck into the bacon and eggs —you'll find them in the fridge. I've got to see quite a few people tomorrow, so you'll have the day to yourself to make the beds and clean up the whole flat. You'll find a hoover in the cupboard. After that, you can get some food in for when we come back and for next day's breakfast—I'll bung you the money before I go. You'll want for nothing here if you play your cards right. Food, board, even a few bob spending money. All right?"

"Er—um—yes, that's fine."

"Good lad! What with parties and preoccupations, this gaff has run to seed a bit. Dust all the furniture now, mind."

"Now I comprehend!" said Maurice with satisfaction. "You've been and got us a valet! Smart work!"

"All this place needed was a valet. What's your surname then, cocky?"

"Prentice," said the bewildered Dave.

"Splendid, Prentice! We'll call you that, an' you call us 'sir'—savvy? I want to do this proper, you see."

"Er—yes."

"Yes *sir*, you mean. Know your place, Prentice."

"Yes sir."

"Fine, fine. I'm sure you're going to settle in splendidly."

Dave did settle in fairly well, although his lowly status was a humiliation. Wonder upon wonders, he became a good worker, basking in the reflected glory of a Coker, and meekly obeying orders in a way that would have astounded every one of his previous employers. The flat was indeed worthy of the nobility, let alone the light-fingered gentry. Once belonging to a wealthy family, now in Rhodesia, it had been left to their aged grandparents to keep up. When the old man died, his widow had let the place in a near-hysterical hurry, for it had too many memories for her. So she fled to a country cousin, leaving the keys with a nice young businessman who, in answer to her advertisement, had paid a lump sum in advance in cash. Frank and his cronies and henchmen had soon drunk the oaken wine cupboard, with its old family flasks, as dry as the proverbial bone, but otherwise they did little damage. No antiques or furniture were sold, for a fox never raids the hen-roost nearest home. So the front room, despite the fierce young men who sprawled around in it, their feet resting on bookshelves or drawers, and despite the thickening dust, retained its period Regency character. The silver stood untouched and unpolished in its glass cases, the Pavilion type settee with gilded legs remained in place, bestrewn with copies of the *News of the World* and the *Greyhound Express*, and the elegant harp stood erect as if awaiting nimble fingers.

Dave soon grew to know each and every object, for Frank quickly became as fussy as a housewife over every speck of dust. It was a huge flat, with steps leading down into an ill-lit servants' quarter where Dave had to make his home, having made a moonlight flit from his old lodgings.

Frank barked orders at him, and insisted on always being called "sir", but otherwise treated him fairly. Maurice, however, couldn't resist drilling poor Dave.

"Hands on head! Hands by your side! Atten-shun! To the kitchen—march!" Maurice would bellow, and Dave would obey, although the "hands on head" tomfoolery was very hurtful to the pitiful remnants of his pride.

If he wanted to go out, he had to ask Frank, who would toss him some small change and fix a time for him to return. Dave comforted himself by thinking that soon they would appreciate him as an equal, and take him along on their various jobs and enterprises.

Alas, every time a job was planned, or illegal activity so much as discussed, it was always the same old story.

" Prentice! "

" Yes sir? "

" You can withdraw now, right? Tidy up the kitchen or somethink. "

" Yes sir. "

" Right then, hoppit and smartish. "

" Yes sir. "

One day Dave thought, they will realise my true worth. As a villain, to tell the truth, he made a very good cook. In fact, years ago as a school leaver he had been an apprentice chef in an hotel, before becoming involved in the great ham-smuggling racket. Thanks to Frank's ignorance of protocol, and to Maurice's slackness, Dave was allowed to sit at table with his employers, once he had served them. Maurice compared Dave with servants of his mother, in their pre-war big house days, but always to Dave's disadvantage. (Maurice had literally driven his mother distracted, and she now dwelt in a Hove nursing home, where nobody visited her.) One frequent guest at the dinner table was Whitey, a henchman of Frank's and a sturdy young man with gruff awkward manners and the blue eyes of a killer. His peculiarity was a completely bald head.

They were all seated at dinner one day, feeling fairly pleased with life, though as a matter of fact they had neglected to say Grace. Whitey, who did not understand about Dave's inferior status, broke an unwritten rule by talking shop in front of him. It was only an innocent and technical comment on house-breaking tools, but it was the lead that Dave was waiting for. For days he had been rehearsing an intellectual speech with which to impress the others, and to show them that he was heart and soul behind them in every illegal move they made.

" Society calls us criminals, " he said darkly " but what made us into villains if not Society? What chance have we ever had, with Society against us all the way? Yet if we fight back at Society, it has the hypocrisy to call us criminals. We are only victims of Society. Society, you see, makes us do the crimes, and yet *we* get the blame. It's really Society what's to blame. "

" Shut up! " shouted Frank angrily, and an awkward silence fell upon the dinner party. Dave was chastened at once, Frank scowled fiercely and the other two seemed more amused than anything else.

" Criminal, isn't it? " said Whitey, nudging Maurice.

" Yes, what'll Society make us do next? " the latter queried.

" Society'll make me poke you one, young Prentice, if you don't get in that kitchen and make the tea, " said Frank.

" Yes sir, " sighed poor Dave, and he shambled off to indulge in a fit of the sulks. Dave's little nonsense-talk had annoyed Frank, for though it didn't exactly mean anything, it touched vaguely upon the moralistic side. As Frank's sense of logic was superior to Dave's, he naturally did not care to think about morals or ethics at all. His own philosophy, as it happens, was that Everyone Looks After Number One. Thus, although he was atrocious enough in all conscience, he was at least spared Dave's twin faults of intense envy and self pity. He looked on himself as a man among men, all out for themselves, and he scorned the doctrine of the underdog.

After tea, Dave was again banished, while the grownups played games. This was no great hardship for Dave, for their games were alarming in the extreme. Frank would bring out some of his collection of Western pistols, and he and his friends would practice drawing on each other. With holsters strapped to their waists, Frank and Maurice would face each other, size each other up and then wham! each would be looking down the muzzle of a pistol. Frank was the quickest off the mark, and his hand and gun seemed to flash into position in the time it takes to blink an eyelid. Frank had no live ammunition on the premises, but Dave did not know this, and whenever he heard Western drawls, his heart sank. Once he had come in with a tray, and both Maurice and Frank had drawn on him simultaneously. The teapot was a goner, and Dave had felt sure his heart would follow suit. Since then he had often been summoned for a similar purpose, and Maurice had even ordered him to play dead. So being in disgrace at least spared him this other humiliation.

Later, the three friends went out to a club, and Dave was left alone to mope. After an hour of such moping, his rebellious Bolshie strain took over. Why shouldn't he too go out and enjoy himself? True he was skint, but he could flog some of the antiques to a feller he knew. Frank would never notice, and in any case, he'd be out until all hours. A further inspiration came his way—why shouldn't he dress up in Frank's smart clothes, as long as he was home first in time to put them back?

Twenty minutes later, he admired himself in front of

the drawing room mirror. He wore a black suit, black tie and a white shirt with large cuffs. In his own estimation he looked splendid, but a seasoned dandy would have had much to say in criticism. For one thing, Dave was taller than Frank, but Frank was broader than Dave. Hence shirt and suit hung upon their new wearer in folds, with the trousers at half mast betraying a glimpse of hairy leg, and the jacket ending somewhere above Dave's tummy, leaving a three inch gap before the trousers began. Just then, the doorknob clicked, and Frank and Maurice returned.

" Too bad the Law showing up like that, " Maurice was saying, " but—Gawd strewth!"

" Stap me, what's this then? " Frank shouted, seeing Dave in the hall. It was very, very fortunate for Dave that he had not yet reached Stage Two of his master plan. If Frank had found him wearing his overcoat, the pockets bulging with candlesticks, there is no knowing what vengeance he might not have taken. As it was, he was none too pleased. He marched Dave back to his room, ordered him to change and then to proceed to the drawing room once more for his trial.

Dave, though quivering with fear, decided to use his ingratiating approach. Years ago, at the age of five, he had perfected this heart-winning routine. At heart Dave was still a five-year-old, as that had been his heyday, with everyone petting him and saying how sweet he was. In those days, he had been good-looking, fair-haired and enchanting. Now he had run to seed, he had lost every semblance of grace or innocence, but when being ingratiating he did not remember this. In his mind's eye, he was a twinkle-eyed child, expecting his innocent-yet-mischievous appearance to melt the stoniest heart. "Who me?" he felt his look implied, as he hopped imploringly from one foot to another, as if about to jump onto Frank's knee and plant a sticky kiss on the other's scarred cheek.

In reality, Dave looked grotesque. He had not shaved for two days, and he had dressed again hurriedly, so that his flannel shirt hung out. His long boney legs were awkwardly constructed for child-like skipping, and his little boy's smile revealed shockingly bad teeth. As for his winsome chuckle, it emerged as a guffaw, and his so-called pleading expression seemed merely fatuous.

"Look at it!" scoffed Maurice. "He thinks he's a puppy that wants his tummy scratched."

"That's it!" snapped Frank. "Well, Prentice, if you can't behave as our valet, you can be our dog. Down on all fours, sir! Go down!"

"What's that, sir?"

"Dogs don't talk. Get on all fours!"

With all the dignity he could muster, Dave complied.

"There's a good dog. Right then. You can do the jobs as before, but when in our company, it's on all fours from now on. I'm not joking, either. Maurice, you do the honours. See if you can house-train this vicious-looking brute."

"Righty-ho, then. Here, boy! Come on!"

On hands and knees, Dave approached, looking pitifully woe-begone. If he had had a tail, it would have been between his legs.

"Right! Roll over! Easy, boy. Now play dead. You want a cigarette? Beg for it, boy. Sit up and beg. Paws up, that's it. Now pant, come on."

"I always kick my dogs," Frank commented. He looked perfectly grave as he said this, but actually his insides were a turmoil of suppressed laughter. A more ludicrous sight than Dave, in mortal fear, sitting up and begging with his tongue hanging out, would be hard to imagine. Maurice put a cigarette in Dave's pocket, and then Frank commanded him to go back to his basket. Silently, Dave shuffled back to his bedroom, still on hands and knees.

"Looks like he's got distemper," Frank commented loudly as he left. "Might have to have him put down—what do you think?"

"Nothing that a dose of flea-powder won't cure."

A week had passed, and the Coker household were at their normal midday meal. Frank and Maurice were doing justice to a large chicken, while Dave the dog waited patiently under the table.

"Here's a bit of leg for you, doggie," said Maurice kindly, passing the tit-bit down into Dave's open mouth. "Say 'woof woof,' then."

"Woof woof," said Dave wondering how he had ever managed to get into such a predicament.

Just then, the 'phone rang, and Frank left the room. Five minutes later he returned, looking solemn, and ordered Dave back to his kennel. With practised ease, Dave made his way back to his room on all fours, reaching up with one paw to turn the door handle. Once inside the room, he reverted to his old self, and lay on the bed smoking and wondering when Frank would appreciate him for his true worth.

" The job's off, " Frank was saying to Maurice.
" That was Whitey's girl, Sheila, to say that he's just
up the 'ospital having stitches put in over 'is eye. 'E's
been midday drinking to get 'is nerve up, an' got in a
scrap with four Paddies along by Norfolk Square.
Just our flaming luck. "

" All planned out to the last detail, too, " moaned
Maurice. " I might never get the chance again. Mind you,
I could hardly believe my ears at the time, when the
guv'nor said to take the cash to the outside safe in the
bank, and gave me the keys. "

" You've got an honest face, that's what it is, Morry
boy. I always had faith in you. Now, maybe I can get
hold of one of the other boys. "

" You're joking! Listen, I've got to *be* there in twenty
effing minutes. S'pose you round up some joker while
the Bingo is on, how will I know his face or that he's
genuine? He might cop the money for himself."

" That's true—better call the whole job off, to be on
the safe side. "

" You're right for once, old son. Seems such a waste,
though. Hold on! Hold on! I have it! Why should we
send Whitey or one of the boys, who'll want fair shares,
when all the time we have someone who'll do it for a pat
on the head and a dog biscuit? "

" You're never thinking what I think you're
thinking. "

" I only am, old squire. Every well trained dog runs
errands for his master. "

" Hmm. Let alone a pat on the head, I reckon that one
was dropped on the head at birth. I reckon *you* must
'ave been, too, to suggest such a thing. Tell the truth, I

was going to bung 'im a fiver an' tell 'im to sod off out of it. We've 'ad our fun with 'im, and I reckon we've pushed 'im beyond the bounds of 'uman sanity. "

" Frank, Frank, money-in-the-bank, just listen! Why do you think he takes it? 'Cos he hero-worships you. I know his type, it's what a college man would call a permanent adolescent. He looks on you the same way a schoolboy looks on Jesse James at the pictures. I knew my education would come in handy. Now, what do you say, old sportsman? We does or we doesn't? Speak now or stay forever shtoom, as I've got to be off to my duties. "

" Oh, Da-ave! " called called Frank in a sing-song tone. " Here, boy. Good doggie! Time for walkies! "

Dave eventually appeared.

" Right, up on your hind feet! " Frank commanded. " You're a man now, you've been promoted. Chief errand boy in chief, we'll call you. What do you say? "

" Thank you, sir, " said Dave gratefully.

" We've done with all that 'sir' mullarkey. You call me Frank—savvy? "

" Yes, Frank, " replied Dave faintly. He was over-whelmed.

" Right, Davey-lad. Listen carefully. There's a Satdy afternoon Bingo session starting in an hour, and ending at ar past six. Compre'end? "

" Er—yes. "

" Good for you! Now, I want you to play Bingo all afternoon, see? I'll bung you the necessary, don't worry. Now, listen carefully. After it's all over, hang about casually. Maurice here won't recognise you, see? He'll walk past you, holding a slim black brief-case. As he takes 'is coat off a hook, he'll put the brief-case down on a chair for a brief moment. Whereupon, you pick it up an' slip it inside a heavy overcoat with which I shall provide you. All clear? Now, be standing near Maurice's coat—it's that one 'e's got on—with *your* coat unbuttoned, all ready. Put the brief-case tightly under your arm and clear off lively-like. Do up your coat outside, and return here in zig-zags, not direct. If there's a hue and cry, don't panic, it'll only be Maurice going into 'is 'I've been robbed' act. I'll be here waiting for you. Got that? "

" Yes, oh yes! Thank you, thank you. "

A passer-by outside the new Bingo hall in Brighton on Saturday, at half past six on a cruel February evening, might have heard a strange uproar issuing from within. Predominant among the babble of voices was one which, in strident tones, boomed out, " I've been robbed! "

Not far away, in the toilet at the Clock Tower, Dave sat in a cubicle turning a black brief-case over and over in his hands. At last, at last! He was triumphant, he was Big Time, he was an honorary Coker! It was almost too good to be true! Wait! Suppose it *was* too good to be true? Suppose it had been merely a test, as part of his apprenticeship, and that the brief-case was really empty of money?

Unable to resist his curiosity, he gave the case a tug, but it seemed to be locked. To make really sure it was locked, he pushed the end of one foot under the strap, pinned the brief-case to the door with his *other* foot, held the lavatory walls tight at each side and kicked his first foot. Thus he discovered that the brief-case was *not* locked. Inside it were several brown paper bags, stapled at the tops, that contained the Bingo takings for Friday and Saturday. Almost without realising it, Dave unstapled one bag, and found it stuffed with banknotes. Satisfied in the quality of his handiwork, Dave tucked the brief-case under his arm and wandered outside.

His nerves felt shattered and he needed a drink. Once inside the dingy brownness of a public bar, he had ordered a half of Sussex bitter before he realised that he had none of his own money on him. As usual when gambling, his luck had been abominable. Nothing to do but dip into the brief-case, though he knew that Frank wouldn't like it.

Awkwardly, he fumbled in the case, not daring to open it too wide. He came up with an elastic banded roll, from which he peeled a oncer and was then immediately hailed by his old friend Bob.

" Don't say you're in the money! " said Bob, his eyes popping. " I don't believe it! "

" Oh yes, I'm—er—a bookie now. Doing all right. "

" What, work for yourself, do you? "

" Oh yes. What're you having? "

" Well, seeing the size of that roll, I'll have a double Scotch. "

" Right you are. Double Scotch, please. "

"Look at this bloke! " said Bob loudly to the barman, pointing at Dave. " It's a real rags-to-riches story. Last time I saw 'im, 'e 'adn't a penny to bless 'imself with, an' now look! 'E's got the stuff in wads! A self-made man, that's what you are, and it does me good to see it. Gives me the strength to go on, as you might say. "

Everyone in the pub seemed interested. Bob had to go

after that, but Dave had already made seventeen new friends. Twelve of these accompanied him to the next pub, where he made an extra fourteen acquaintances. Obeying Frank's instructions to the letter, Dave returned home in zig zags. To be quite truthful, he never reached home, as he collapsed on the pavement within two pubs of his base. A policeman approached, and Dave's entourage of Irishmen and Scotsmen quickly faded away.

Dave lay down in a blissful sleep, overjoyed at having found so much Christian good fellowship in the world. He still clutched his precious briefcase. The policeman looked down on him tolerantly. This, after all, made a nice change from hysterical Bingo hall managers. He prodded Dave with his boot.

"Wake up down there," he ordered. "Are you all right? Whereabouts do you live?"

Dave woke up with a start and looked at the policeman in stricken horror. He had been caught, nicked and captured! Somebody had grassed!

"My Gawd, my Gawd, it wasn't me," he wailed sitting up. "I never done it, I never been near the Bingo hall! It was that Maurice, I tell you! He give me the bag! It was 'is idea, I swear! I never knew what was in it till I opened it, like."

"You've 'ad too much, sir. Can you find your way home?"

"That's right, I've never been near the Bingo, nor never met Maurice. I've been dreaming!" gasped Dave, who indeed at that moment could not tell his head from his heels. However, by now the penny had dropped. This last statement could be interpreted literally, for

Dave picked up the wrong end of the briefcase, and all the money fell out.

A moment later, the policeman spoke briskly into his radio, for he was fully automated, and emitted electric robot-like crackles as he walked his beat. Not long after that, a car arrived.

So, just as Maurice and the Bingo hall manager were leaving Brighton police station, a constable ran out and called them back. Maurice and Dave were then confronted.

" I think you two have met, " said the Inspector, who was not without a sense of humour.

For the sake of those sensitive souls who shrink from all mention of pain and unpleasantness, a veil will be drawn over the two years following the arrests of Dave and Maurice. Frank, it may be mentioned, was not implicated at all in the Bingo conspiracy, and continued in business, going from strength to strength as if leading a charmed life.

As our veil is lifted once more, we see our heroes in a very different set of circumstances. Ozzie was out and about for one thing, and going straight at that. He was a successful under-manager-cum-bouncer of an amusements hall. On one occasion he had been fined ten pounds for breaking an admittedly vicious young man's head open with an iron bar, but the *Evening Argus* wrote this up most favourably, with even a small photograph. The incident had taken place inside the amusements hall, and Ozzie therefore looked smugly upon it as a blow for Law and Order.

Two doors away from Ozzie's place of employment stood the brightly painted and widely advertised "Jamboree Club". Here could be found the remainder of our heroes, and with heroes like these, what need have we for villains?

Maurice's term at Pentonville had so distressed his mother that the unfortunate lady had departed this life altogether. Maurice duly inherited, and it is to Frank's credit that he stopped his old friend, when again he saw him, from drinking himself to death altogether. While celebrating his good fortune at a houseboat party in Shoreham Harbour, Maurice took it into his head to dive overboard fully clothed and enjoy a moonlight swim. In his bemused condition, he dived from the wrong side of the boat onto the wharf and broke his leg. Visiting him in hospital, Frank persuaded him into a partnership, cheques were duly signed and the Jamboree Club came into being.

Upstairs, in a madly flamboyant penthouse, Frank and Maurice lived the lives of Turkish pashas, and all quite legally too. The club's licence had been granted in the name of an unconvicted friend of Maurice's, who took a small fee and then went to Ireland. To use Frank's own expression, he and Maurice were "coining a mint", for the club was very popular among wealthy businessmen from the near East and Eastern Europe.

This can be explained in part by the entertainment offered. Apart from a small Greek orchestra, this consisted of several wickedly beautiful young ladies, all scantily dressed, who were the paid hostesses. These would pout and flirt and caress, whispering both promises and also requests for the most expensive chicken and champagne.

Later, as the customers departed, the girls followed suit. What they did in their off-duty hours was no concern at all of either Frank or Maurice. Each of those worthies would be equally shocked at any suggestion of immorality at the Jamboree Club. However, any hostess who did *not* comply with the customers' wishes, however far from the club premises the refusal took place, would find herself at first cautioned and finally dismissed.

To descend to lesser fry—Whitey was the barman and Dave was one of the washers-up. Somewhat ruffled and embittered by his experiences in Wormwood Scrubs, Dave had presented himself, performed his ingratiating act, and been hired at once by Frank in honour of his sheer cool cheek. Grumbling constantly, Dave settled in and worked adequately.

Frank, Maurice and a select bunch of their cronies still enjoyed their old shoot-about games, but now with a difference added. Frank was now confident enough to use live bullets in his own pistol, and he could seemingly hit any target. While customers on the ground floor drank and danced, muffled explosions from upstairs could be heard through the swirl of the music. Soon, Frank's gun room was perforated with bullet holes, and Frank himself would impress friends and select guests by shooting a playing card from Maurice's far from steady hand. This was the culmination of an ambition that had begun way back in Frank's Teddy Boy days. He had, so long ago, examined his first pistol admiringly in a telephone booth and promptly shot himself in the hand. At the hospital, the police had called at his bedside and enquired as to who had shot him. No prints had been found on the gun, which was covered in blood, so

Frank had blamed a big black man. Sundry Negroes had been located, and when restored to health, Frank had been invited to pick out his would-be assassin. He got out of it by explaining that all coloured men looked the same to him, and the matter was dropped.

Now an expert in what he called "trigger-nometry", Frank was frequently featured in the local press as a loveable, dashing, romantic and eccentric Brighton personality. Dave shuddered when he heard the bangs, but he was subjected to no further humiliations, for in the tide of their success, neither Frank nor Maurice paid him any attention whatsoever. Instead of being grateful, Dave brooded upon this.

If it wasn't for me, he thought, Maurice would never have gone inside and his old lady would never have snuffed it. So, Dave concluded, the whole rise of the Jamboree Club was really of his own making. And what did he get? Well, actually he got seven pounds a week, all meals, and no insurance stamps, with time off for signing on and drawing his dole. Many would be grateful for these privileges, but Dave for one was not, and he considered that Frank and Maurice had "sold out to Society".

Dave did not know it, but his ideas on Society were now quite unfashionable, for a side-effect of the Labour government keeping too many of its promises was that Socialism was being discredited. Mysticism was now all the rage, and one of the most popular of the hostesses at the Jamboree Club was an eager devotee of this latest cloak for restless ignorance.

This hostess was named Brenda, and she was ravishingly and meltingly beautiful. She had long, wavy brown hair, with a glorious sheen to it, and dark eyes like mysterious forest pools. Her lips were well shaped and so was the rest of her. Off duty and on, she wore such a minutely short skirt, revealing sensible woollen panties, that many of her friends accused her of trying to drive men frantic. Brenda indignantly denied this charge, for she seemed genuinely unaware of the effect that she had upon men. A very strange girl, she had a small mentally afflicted child with a large head.

"You can see my little girl is going to be brainy with all that head," Brenda would say proudly. "She's bound to go to university, you can see."

Spellbound, her ever-present male audience would agree, even though the child was seven years old and could not yet speak. Brenda's smart flat was always full of young men, who baby-sat for her, and attended to most of the housework. Completely oblivious to the fact that these willing servants were all madly in love with her, she would talk to them only of spiritual matters, which did indeed drive them nearly frantic. With admirable self-control, they would discuss God with her while forcibly repressing the urges of the Devil. To make matters worse, Brenda would sit on their laps in turn, and caress them absently while expounding some point of Spiritualist doctrine. No one had ever known her to sleep with anyone, but there was always hope. Her company drove the already cranky young men crankier and crankier. They were mostly neat and obsessive would-be poets, living in digs and working as clerks or bus conductors. Although mostly religious, their Church was built not upon a rock but upon the shifting sands of fashion. With enormous solemnity, they would expound their gospel of the moment, as laid down by some guru or show business personality. None of them had studied the organised religions of the world very deeply, or had indeed read any book from cover to cover, but this did not stop them from laying down the law on matters of Life, Death and Eternity. As they gazed yearningly at Brenda, their endless babble of "vibrations", "astral planes" and "spirit guides" would carry an increasingly hysterical note.

For many months after her arrival in Brighton, Brenda did no work whatsoever, but vaguely told her hangers-on that the Lord would provide. What the Lord did provide was actually fat Jewish or Persian entrepreneurs, who showered gold lavishly until they realised that no payment was forthcoming. One of these worthies, when disillusioned with Brenda, had the perception to recognise that her unusual talents made her an ideal hostess for the Jamboree Club.

Frank briefly outlined her duties to her, set her to work the same day, and was gratified to notice her popularity. Recognising no such thing as evil, even when in its midst, Brenda would question the shady businessmen about their souls. Most of them had never realised that they *had* souls, and they were at first repentant of their more base desires, then intrigued and finally completely captivated. Soon they flocked in night after night, and treated Brenda with huge respect as a kind of a priestess to whom they made Confession. While she accepted this role with her customary unflappability, she had cause to complain to Whitey about her constant diet of chicken and champagne.

" Ask for vodka, then, and I'll give you water, "
Whitey obliged.

One evening, Brenda was amiably going about her
tasks, sitting on the knee of a stout customer and giving
him religious instruction.

" Oy, mine liddle vun, you think I have a soul? "
queried the customer. " Vat vill of me become ven I
die, then tell me. "

" There is no such thing as death, only a change, "
Brenda replied.

" Ah, but vat a change! Such drastic change as that
I can do vithout already! How can I to mine friends
explain der change that haff come over me, hey mine
liddle vun? "

" You silly man! You can always make new friends in
the Spirit World. "

" Ah, but mine Brenda, it is here below that I am new
friends in need of making, mine pretty vun. Vill you not
come to my flat and ve can drink to friendship? "

" Oh you! You know I never go home with customers.
When I finish here, I need my sleep. " While the customer
accepted this meekly, another person did not. This was
a rival hostess, a hard faced young call-girl who was
jealous of Brenda. She reported to Frank that Brenda did
not go with the customers, and this amazed both Frank
and Maurice, who had both misinterpreted the new
hostess's popularity.

" I'll tell Whitey to speak to her about it tomorrow, "
Frank promised. Whitey was never one to beat about
the bush.

" You're expected, if you work here, to have sex with
the customers, " he explained to Brenda next day. " We

can't force you, 'cos that's procuring. We can't provide accomodation, 'cos that's brothel keeping. Frank and Maurice both want their business to be completely above board and completely respectable, so if you can't make your own arrangements about sex, they'll have to fire you. All right?"

" Oh really, Whitey, the things you say! You are funny! Do you believe in Spiritualism?"

" See here Brenda, I . . . " and his voice trailed away as his eyes met hers and she flashed him one of her Looks.

" I—er—I dunno," he continued huskily. " Funny thing happened to me once. When I was quite a young kiddie I got arf kicked to death in a punch-up at Grimsby Fish Dock, up north. Proper done over I was, an' left for dead. Truth of the matter was, I *was* dead. There I was somewhere in the air an' I looked down an' there was me, Whitey, lying on the deck. Funny feeling, really. I seemed to sense some kind of a Being beside me, but I didn't want no part of it. I've always been a scrapper, you see Brenda, so you might say I fought with Death. With a great deal of pain and trouble I got down inside of myself again. By then the ambulance 'ad come anyway. Do you know, Brenda, I've never told anyone that right up till now! What was I talking about before?"

" I don't know. Let me tell you about spirit guides and the astral plane."

" I don't want to know about that! My parents were decent Church of England, and if guardian Angels and Heaven were good enough for them, they're good enough for me. You're only doing what I might call putting good old wine into ugly new bottles."

Brenda herself was surprised at the depths she had found in the unpleasant-looking Whitey. Whitey was equally surprised at himself. Tamely, he allowed Brenda to rattle on about mediums, seances and people keeping contact with friends and relations on the Other Side.

"I don't hold with it," he said at length. "It's not healthy, and the Bible forbids it. What's more I don't believe the spirits that are called up are the right ones at all. They're low, coarse spirits, much like I'll be, and they've been earthbound for the duration. Just 'cos they're dead don't mean to say they are all-wise or all-virtuous. In my opinion, they're having the mediums on, pretending to be people's Dads and Aunties just for the hell of it, to pass the time. It's definitely wrong, and I'm surprised at you, Brenda. No wonder Frank told me to give you a telling-off."

Annoyed and confused, Whitey reported back to Frank and Maurice.

"Well?" asked the latter. "What did she say? You were talking long enough."

"No joy, guv'nor. She wouldn't listen."

"My life, it was *you* that was listening from what I could see. All right, I'll handle this." Heavy-handedly, Maurice called Brenda over to a quiet table.

"I've been hearing complaints about you," he said sternly. Brenda gave him a dazzling smile. Twenty minutes later, they parted, with a promise from Brenda that she would go out with Maurice next Tuesday.

"It's no use talking to her," Maurice reported back to Frank. "She's some kind of religious maniac."

"Well, we're opening now. I'll talk to her about it tomorrow—she won't come any of that nonsense with me. I'm surprised at you, Maurice—you're getting too soft."

So it was that the next day, Frank and Brenda sat down for a heart-to-heart talk, during the course of which the barrier between Management and Labour broke down entirely. Frank, informed that he had a soul, roared with laughter and patted Brenda's hand in a wise and understanding fashion. Somehow the notion seemed to tickle his funny-bone. He even went so far as to recite a poem:

"Last night I had a dream, that to Heaven I
    did go,
Where was it that I came from, they wanted for
    to know.
I said, 'I come from Brighton,' and Saint Peter
    gave a stare.
He said 'Come in, Frankie Coker, you're the first
    we've had from there.'"

At this Brenda giggled heartily, and gave Frank a coy slap. They agreed to go out on the town together on the following Wednesday.

A strange situation had thus arisen, for Maurice and Frank were now rivals, and so they cooled off one another considerably. Brenda would not commit herself bodily (so to speak) to either one, and her flirtatious ways and her habit of delivering sermons at incongruous moments were enough to keep the emotions of the two club owners at fever pitch. Not liking to admit weakness, their quarrels were not about Brenda, but about money. Frank had long ago taken charge of the financial side, for he was the more responsible party. They had a joint bank account, but in fact it was Frank who wrote all the cheques and gave Maurice whatever he asked for. However, now that Maurice needed money to take Brenda out, Frank began to get niggly and to claim that they must go easy on spending for the sake of the business. Naturally, Maurice did not like this, and harsh words were exchanged.

Far away from their penthouse, deep in the squalor of the kitchen, Dave soon became aware of his employers' differences. Prison had not done Dave very much good. His boyishness was diminished and his bitterness was increased. He wondered how to use the rift for his own benefit. Inwardly, he blamed himself for ruining his chances as henchman to Frank, by his disastrous handling of the Bingo job. Perhaps now that Frank was a bit distraught, he could slip into his favours once again.

The opportunity came unexpectedly one morning, when he was asked to take Frank up a cup of tea. Rehearsing gestures of friendship, he ascended the stairs, knocked on Frank's door and entered on command.

" Oh, it's *you* is it, chief? " said Frank, who was sitting on the edge of the bed feeling fed up. The day before he had spent pounds buying Brenda a new coat, and the minute he had got in, Maurice piped up for money to buy a new car with. He had told Maurice off both obscenely and curtly, and now he felt a little ashamed. Dave's gangling figure didn't make him feel any better.

" It's a bugger, isn't it? " said Dave, sympathetically, putting the cup down. " Still, at least this tea's better than what you've been used to in the past, when you're inside, I mean. I bet you've done more time than arf the blokes in Brighton put together. "

Frank looked up at Dave balefully. To tell the truth,

they were somewhat at cross-purposes. In retrospect, Dave gloried in his prison sentences, as if each one was a praiseworthy recommendation. Whereas Frank seldom spoke of his bits of trouble, and regarded arrest and imprisonment as the results of error, stupidity and shameful bad management. To boast of such waste and miscalculation, as Dave did with pride, was to Frank the biggest folly of them all. Silently, he hoped that Dave would go away.

Encouraged, Dave continued.

" Of course, " he prattled on, " what chance have the likes of us got against Society? We—— "

At this point, Frank threw a shoe at him, and he fled. Downstairs, in a terrible rage, he smashed two plates on purpose, by hurling them on the floor. Maurice at once appeared, so Dave apologised and swept up the pieces.

" For Gawd's sake be careful, " Maurice admonished him. " We've got enough money troubles as it is."

" You can always get more money, though, can't you? " Dave ventured.

" Where from? Trees? "

" Oh—er—um, I thought you and Frank did jobs, like. "

" No, what gave you that idea? We haven't done for ages. Frank's always been set on going straight, he tells me. "

" Just 'cos Frank's gone soft, don't mean to say that you have to as well, " replied Dave, taking a liberty.

" Watch your mouth, you! You're only a washer-up, not the bleedin' Mafia. Matter of fact, Frank and I work together, so if *he* lays off the jobs, *I* lays off the jobs. Savvy? "

" Well, if you don't mind me saying, you could easily go out on your own. You could borrow one of Frank's pistols and stick up a bank or something. "

"Dave, get on with your work and don't talk so much."

" Well, you could though, couldn't you? "

At that moment, the 'phone rang in the next room and Maurice departed. It was Brenda ringing to ask if Maurice could take her out that afternoon.

"No money, honey, " he replied, and rang off.

On an impulse, he then rapidly made his way to the room where Frank was wont to keep his shooting-irons. He had never done a job on his own before, but only taken part in Frank's carefully planned out operations, when his role was that of a cog in a machine. Suddenly he was filled with anger at Frank's paternalism, and at Frank's virtually taking over his inheritance. Now he would prove his independence, and start a private bank account of his own, from whence he could draw as much as he liked to treat Brenda and to treat himself.

" Who does he think he is? " Maurice muttered, as he found an old Western pistol (which Frank had lovingly restored to working order), and clumsily loaded it with the appropriate bullets. The gun was a Smith and Wesson, one of a pair that usually hung crossed upon the wall. Maurice placed it in the pocket of his overcoat and set out on his mission. Unthinkingly following Frank's "fox and hen roost" theory, he took a bus somewhere out into the industrial backwoods that start at Portslade and sweep on as far as the very hills where Lancing College stands as a majestic landmark against the wild and haunting Downs, whose rounded crests were now flecked with snow. He and Frank did share a car, but he preferred not to use it, for it was open-topped, with jet-like rear wings and painted lilac and white, with soft scarlet lining. In addition, it was as big as the cabin cruiser it resembled, and it was the recognised trade mark of the Jamboree Club, advertisements for which were plastered all over it. In short, not wholly ideal for a quick and easy getaway.

The staff at a sleepy little bank, housed in a comfortable old building that looked like a sweet shop, were mildly surprised at the noisy, fussy entrance of a tubby, perky little fat man, who looked as though he'd been drinking. As indeed he had.

" All right, let's be having you! " this presumed customer announced, darting his head from side to side with bright, starling-like stares, and rapidly rubbing his hands together. Seeing that each of the two clerks were serving previous comers, he chose the small queue which led up to a neat, pleasant-faced young man in a grey suit. The other queue, you see, led up to a fierce spinsterish lady who looked like a schoolmistress.

" Come on, come on, haven't got all day! " barked the newcomer, half humorously, half irritably. At last his turn arrived.

" Well sir, what can we do for you? " enquired the clerk politely.

Maurice, for it was he, levelled his gun at the clerk's nose. The clerk gaped. Often he had mentally rehearsed this moment, for he was an imaginative lad, but now it had arrived he felt spellbound, as if witnessing a miracle.

" Hand over your greens, " Maurice hoarsely

whispered. " Give me all the notes you've got handy, and I'll call it a day. If you leave your post, I'll shoot. Come on, you gone to sleep or something? Look lively! "

Only one customer was now present, a middle-aged housewife anxiously presenting a cheque on which she had forged her husband's name. She was being served by the schoolmistressly clerk.

" Ooh, look! " she said, noticing Maurice's gun. " What's that fellow up to? He's got a gun, I do believe. He must be a bank robber. "

" Good heavens, you're right! Do just hang on a moment. "

The schoolmistress, who had never been known to lose her head, did not lose it now. She could see that young Roger was frozen in a kind of trance, for the gun-barrel acted upon him as a snake against a rabbit. This disconcerted Maurice, who wanted the money quickly, and who never seriously contemplated shooting the boy. Just as he decided he ought to shoot at the ceiling to snap the boy out of it, the schoolmistress took charge.

" What, " she enquired tartly, " do you think you're playing at? Put down that silly gun at once, do you hear? "

Maurice turned to her, aggrieved.

" Look, lady. I'm only doing my job, " he explained, as if appealing to reason. " I can't seem to get through to this lad. Will you serve me? "

The schoolmistress looked towards the money drawer, and noticed that young Roger's finger was resting on the alarm button.

" Do you want notes? " she enquired, opening the drawer.

" That's more my language you're talking! " smirked Maurice, putting the pistol back in his pocket and holding out an eager hand.

At once, the schoolmistress pinched Roger's leg, he gave a jump and pressed the button and all hell was let loose. The noise was fearful, and clerks in back-rooms dropped their cups of tea and tumbled forth to see what was up.

" Get down! " the schoolmistress told Roger, but the spell being broken, that youth was hot to prove his manhood and vaulted over the counter to tackle Maurice. Maurice wheeled round, waving his pistol. For one second the pistol pointed at the errant housewife — then it moved on. God, as has often been pointed out, moves in a mysterious way His wonders to perform. In that one second, the housewife vowed to reform, and when she saw that Maurice had fled, she looked on it as a judgement, and tore her cheque to pieces. I hope that all you housewives note this incident well.

Maurice had fled, it is true, but the intrepid Roger flew after him in close pursuit. Down the road they ran, with passers by taking up the chase as in an old fashioned hue and cry. At the corner, an old boozing crony of Maurice's lounged against a wall as he studied the racing results. Maurice pounded past, amid wild shouts of " Stop thief. " He waved his pistol as he ran, and the sporting character looked up.

" 'Lo, Maurice, " he said.

" 'Lo, John, " puffed Maurice, saluting him with his pistol and racing on. John returned to his newspaper.

Maurice, meanwhile, decided to elude his pursuers by jumping on a bus. He hurried upstairs, put the gun back in his pocket, and sat looking out of the window. The crowd ran on, then stopped and looked at the bus questioningly.

" Why aren't we moving? " Maurice asked a fellow passenger.

" The driver's not in. "

" Oh my Gawd, " and Maurice hurried downstairs and walked quickly down the road, staring at his feet. However, a cry of " There he is! " forced him to quicken his pace, and he found himself facing a railway station. Ah! Now if a bus was too slow, he could try a train. Inspired by this happy thought, he bounded onto the platform and began to look up the destinations board.

Porter O'Sullivan eyed him suspiciously. Had he got a ticket?

" Stop that man! Hold him! " shouted the worthy Roger, racing onto the platform. This confirmed Porter O'Sullivan's suspicions, for the burly exile mistakenly supposed Roger to be a new clerk from the booking office. As Maurice, with a wild look at Roger, ran pell-mell towards the bridge to Platform Two, he was held by a vice-like grip. Porter O'Sullivan had an especial down on ticket-dodgers, whom he considered to be the lowest of the low.

" Well done! " shouted a dozen voices, as the rest of the crowd caught up. The police had now picked up the trail, and before the slow-thinking Porter had realised it, Maurice was in handcuffs and his own massive hands were being shaken by all and sundry.

Later, the Porter was to receive a reward of twenty

pounds and a medal for courage displayed over and beyond the call of duty.

" I always knew we were right to leave the County Wexford and strike out after our fortunes, " his wife told him afterwards.

" Ah, but if I'd known he had a loaded gun on him, I would have run a mile. "

" Ah, Patrick, it's too modest that you are. "

None of which interesting events and domestic conversation was to be of any use to Maurice whatsoever.

Frank Coker sat at the table in his own club, feeling bitter and gloomy. The cloistral atmosphere of the room may have contributed to his mood, for as he had not yet opened up, the lights were not on, and as always, all the windows were curtained in heavy blue velvet. However, this was not Frank Coker's only reason to be despondent, for he had reached the point where he could only be happy if Brenda was by his side. The day before, he had proposed to her, but she had vaguely refused him, saying that she didn't want to be tied down just yet. She had promised to 'phone him that morning, to say what time she would be meeting him that day. He didn't fancy popping down to her place, as the sight of the dithering namby-pamby youths telling each other that Jesus was an astronaut from Venus made him want to commit mayhem.

Now it will have been supposed that Frank was alone with his brooding thoughts, but this was far from the case. No, his brother Ozzie was actually with him, talking rapidly and cheerfully in the most amusing manner. Yet for all Frank cared at that moment, Ozzie himself might have been upon the planet Venus, where he would presumably be deified by the inhabitants and his space helmet mistaken for a halo, as some of Brenda's friends would have believed.

"So we definitely found this bloke was a copper's nark," Ozzie was saying. "So next time 'e come round, Big Ernie says to 'im, 'me an' Ozzie an' the boys is doin' a bank job tomorrow. Want to come in on it?' 'I might,' 'e says, an' then Ernie goes into all details. 'Changed me mind,' the little nark says, but 'e's quivering with excitement. 'Well, see you,' Big Ernie says. 'See you,' the nark replies, and all agog, 'e runs round the corner to the nearest 'phone box to call up the law an' tell 'em the juicy bit 'o news. No sooner, I said no *sooner*, 'ad 'e 'ad time to dial one number when 'e looks up an' there we was, all eight of us, eyeing 'im froo the glass. We was smoking and blowing the smoke up, wiv our eyes all slits, you know—the frighteners. Reggie was running 'is finger along 'is shiv. So this poor little mush comes out, an' 'e goes on 'is knees, I'm not kidding, 'e frew 'imself on our mercy, 'is tears coming down like buckets. 'Sorry, boys,' 'e says. '*Sorry*?' says Big Ernie. '*Sorry*? I should fink you're sorry.' An' 'e picks the little nark up an' shakes 'im up an' down. You know, Big Ernie's six foot nine an' 'e does weight lifting. Finally 'e puts the nark down quite tenderly, an' 'e says, 'You silly little man. Now go 'ome an' tell your muvver you won't do it no more. An' don't let me see you round 'ere again.' The little nark's thankin' 'im an' sobbing, an' then 'e runs off before Ernie changes 'is mind. Now my point is this—don't you think Big Ernie'd make a good bouncer here? He's down on 'is luck."

" I thought he did that warehouse job last week," said Frank wearily. Ozzie made him feel old.

" No, I told you. Reggie done 'im out of the money. Reggie sold the stuff, an' 'im an' Big Ernie wen' up to London. At Victoria Station, Big Ernie says ' all right, let's 'ave my share.' Reggie agrees, but 'e just 'as to pop down the toilet. Now, the toilet at Victoria's in a basement wiv stairs at each end, like. Reggie goes down one lot o' stairs, leavin' Big Ernie waiting, an' then 'e nips up the other stairs and disappears wiv all the money. Same's a rabbit in one hole an' out of anuvver 'un. So when me and the boys see Reggie, we're gonna do 'im over."

At one time conversation such as this was meat and drink to Frank. Now it made him feel bilious. Looking up, he saw Dave in the doorway, dusting and eavesdropping, and he called him over.

"Didn't I hear the 'phone down here when I was in bed?" he enquired. " Who was it?"

" It was only Brenda 'phoned up to talk to Maurice," said Dave maliciously.

" To *Maurice*? Where *is* Maurice?"

" E went out soon after—I dunno where to."

" I see. All right, hop it."

Dave hopped it, noticing his employer's thunderous countenance with glee. Frank had humiliated *him*, and now, having found Frank's weakness, he could humiliate Frank.

" Where's Maurice?" Whitey suddenly called out

from upstairs, in all innocence. " He was s'posed to be telling me what stock to order. "

" Oh, I 'spect he's out with that Brenda! " Dave shouted back, seeing his chance. " They're very fond of each other. You wannoo 'ear how Brenda talks about 'im—Maurice this and Maurice that! I think there was talk of them two gettin' married, I don't know. Funny pair they'd make—'er all young an' gorgeous an' 'im all old and fat. Still, 'e thinks the world of 'er, buys 'er anything she wants. "

" Get on with your work! " roared Frank, the thunder breaking into a storm. Dave did so. Ozzie left for the amusements arcade soon afterwards, and Frank was left with his thoughts, which were mostly centred around Maurice's unexpected disappearance. Hours went by, and Maurice did not return.

Finally, Brenda turned up, looking complacent. She *was* playing somewhat of a double game with Frank and Maurice, but she meant no harm, never having committed herself to either one. This was simply her natural way of getting money with which to keep herself and her helpless child. To her, all men were simply naughty children, placed on earth to be humoured and to give her jewellery which she could sell. As she went forward to kiss Frank, her ruby lips were curved in almost a motherly smile.

Frank stepped back from her embrace, glaring at her with hatred.

" Get back from me, you slag! " he said, with a dangerous calm. " Don't come here with your lies. I know where you've been and who you've been with! "

" Frank darling, what *are* you talking about? "

" Darling, is it now? That's good, that is. You and
Maurice know what I'm talking about. Where is 'e
now—ashamed to show 'is face, I suppose? "

" Maurice? How should I know? I haven't seen
Maurice all day. "

" Er, scooz me, Frank, " butted in Whitey at that
moment. " But someone's been playing with your guns
and I think he's knocked off one of them. "

Swearing horribly, Frank ran to his gun-room. Yes
indeed, one of his pistols was missing, one of a pair that
he prized. This was the last straw, and Frank was now at
boiling point. Meditatively he toyed with the remaining
pistol, noticing that it was still loaded from one of his
wilder games. Brenda ran into the room, chattering
away about Maurice, and on a momentary impulse,
Frank took aim and fired. The explosion was deafening,
and Brenda fell to the ground with a shriek. Frank fired
at her again as she lay, and then put the pistol in his mouth
and squeezed the trigger. Nothing happened, so with a
curse he looked for his bullets, but they were gone. The
next second, Whitey threw himself at Frank, and brought
the latter down on the floor, where they tussled horribly,
each seeking a strangle hold. Finally, Frank won the
advantage and as he nearly throttled Whitey, he hissed,
" There's no more bullets, you fool. I'm all right—let's
see to Brenda. "

Whitey stood up and spat blood, and together they
looked at Brenda in silence. Even as Whitey knelt to
take her pulse, he knew that it was no good. Brenda was
presumably now a part of the spirit world with which
she had for so long sought contact. Frank lifted her onto
the couch, and told Whitey to telephone the police.

In death, Brenda looked more beautiful than ever. Her calm face was pale, cold and waxlike, and notwithstanding the gruesome condition of her body, Frank bent over her and kissed her forehead.

Before Whitey could reach the 'phone, the police had arrived to question Frank about Maurice, who was safely in custody. When Whitey explained the circumstances, the constables became rather nervous, but they had no reason to be. Entering the gun-room, they found Frank kneeling by the side of the couch, in silence. Those who did not know him better would have believed him to be praying.

And so our story of life upon the southern coast of England must drift into some kind of a conclusion. Both Frank and Maurice are still far from the public eye, in widely separated penal institutions under the indirect surveillance of Her Majesty the Queen. Ozzie is as yet basking in the glory of the now twice exalted and magnified name of Coker. However, certain gentlemen —no name, no uniform—do not believe that he can enjoy this freedom for very much longer. Whitey and Dave are still at their old posts in the Jamboree Club, which is now under new management and renamed "The Plutocrat".

The new owner of the Plutocrat is not a very nice sort of person. Upon taking command, she put an entrance fee of five shillings on the gun-room, advertising it by word of mouth as the very room where the sensational murder was committed. A scrawny gin-soaked woman, with too much make-up, she now struts around the room pointing out the " Exact spot " where Brenda fell, and showing the gaping oafish visitors the " bullet holes where the bullets went right through and out the other side. " This demonstration is easily made, for the whole room is riddled with bullet holes.

And Brenda? Surely there is little to be said of any further activity upon *her* part? Ah, but you have under-estimated the bizarrity of Brighton, a town which has been a talking point for scandal ever since the days of Mrs Fitzherbert. For if certain eyewitnesses at the Plutocrat Club, including that woman who owns it, are to be believed, then Brenda does not rest in peace. Vases move strangely, and plates and cutlery hurl themselves against the wall. However, since a clergyman presided over the much publicised exorcism ceremony, things have been much more peaceful. Even so, neither Dave nor the person known as Big Ernie will sleep on the premises, each claiming to have seen a mysterious "something" emerge threateningly from the fruit-machine. Whether it is Brenda trying in vain to "take it with her", it is hard to say, but Whitey has his own theory. He claims that the spirit is not that of Brenda at all, but a restless emanation from Dave himself, unconsciously created by the latter's twisted mind—in fact, a poltergeist. This theory will be cherished by the sentimentalists who wish to picture Brenda taking her ease on a heavenly cloud in a land of glorious splendour.

Brenda's child continues to exist, and despite her newly hygienic surroundings, can now speak a few words of English.

Only Dave, old reliable Dave, is much the same as ever. Still he grins and dances in his small-boy act, and still he blames "Society" for his misdeeds and short-comings. He now finds a ready sympathiser with this point of view in the Psychiatric Social Worker whom he visits twice weekly. This happy arrangement took place following Dave's arrest on a charge of stealing a van. Smiling impishly, he had told the magistrate that he took the van " because it looked so lonely. " Immediately, the gyves were struck from his wrists and he was handed into the tender care of the aforementioned Psychiatric Social Worker. So far, Dave has been told that he breaks the law because he hates his mother, was thwarted by his father, beaten by his sister, misunderstood by his employers and because, in infancy, he was unscientifically toilet-trained. All of these explanations suit Dave to a tee, and he is as ruefully happy as anyone so martyred can be. And if, with Jeremy Bentham, we believe that democracy is "the greatest happiness of the greatest number", then Dave's state of self-centred bliss is indeed a signpost towards a most remarkable and progressive Future.

The Story of David

For another hopeful writer—
                SUSAN McCRACKEN

Then all cried with one accord,
" Thou art King, and Law, and Lord;
Anarchy, to thee we bow,
Be thy name made holy now! "

And Anarchy the skeleton
Bowed and grinned to every one
As well as if his education
Had cost ten millions to the nation.

Shelley, *The Masque of Anarchy*

Turn back the hands of time to the early 'sixties and make a slight alteration in the latitude and longitude, and we find ourselves upon the upper reaches of the River Tyne, in the environs of a small industrial town. Far away in the shimmering distance, as seen from the highest point in that town, the "new castle", Castle Garth, stood black, gaunt and squat, and containing in its dingy stone hall, the fading colours of the Barons of the North. In David Holt's home town, however, the nearest thing to a castle was the municipal gasworks. Mr Holt, his father, had been a carpenter for most of his life, and they lived in one of the many rows of small brick terraced houses that fronted onto the river. These houses were *not* begrimed with soot, as older northern dwellings are popularly supposed to be, but were of clean red brick. A narrow cobbled alley separated the back yards of each row, and fortunately for the district's children, each of these alleys was wide enough to allow a soap-box cart to pass thundering on its way. The yards themselves were protected on either side of each alley by a brick wall with wooden latched doors inset at regular intervals. In many of these yards, pigeons or rabbits were kept, but the shed in the Holts' yard was full of wood and carpentry tools, some of the latter being heirlooms inscribed with the family name, handed down from long-ago village days. These, although indispensable to any woodcarver, could no longer be bought for love or money.

The evening sunlight streamed through the small lace-curtained windows of the front parlour, played upon the potted fern on the window sill, and slanted across the minutely floral patterned wallpaper hung with many a gaudy shop-bought ornament purchased by Mrs Holt. Poor Mrs Holt had died of cancer some years before, and as the custom of showy funerals was now frowned on as "common", she had been hurried from the Methodist chapel to her plot in the forlorn coarse-grassed cemetery with the minimum of fuss. Mr Holt alone had reared the two boys through adolescence, and had proudly seen his eldest son into the carpentry trade. Henry was apprenticed as a turner, but though quite skilful, he was ashamed of his status as a working man in an academic world. Old Mr Holt could never understand this, for his own ambition had been to be a respected craftsman. He could not see that in this mechanised age, craftsmanship seemed quite outlandish to a younger generation. Henry sought the company of clerks and technical students, whom he was ashamed to bring home, and when his apprenticeship was over, he left town to go on a teacher's training course. Now he lived a gay bachelor's life in Newcastle, working as a woodwork teacher in a shiny new school, with shiny new plug-in equipment.

Mr Holt often shook his head over this, and he did so on this occasion, as a part of his farewell speech to his younger son, David, who was going away to university.

" I can't understand the lad, " he said, as they both sat in that small front parlour drinking warm bottled brown ale. " There he's ashamed to be a carpenter, yet he's pleased as punch to be teaching *other* lads to be carpenters. Now, ordinarily-like, I'd be right proud to have a son who was a teacher, but I did want *someone* to carry on with the carpenter's trade. *You* was to be the one with book-learning, that's what I thought. One time, you know, lad, I'd ha' been the envy of the street if you'd been a teacher. But look now! Any fool can be a teacher now, it seems, but you, you've hit the jackpot going to university! If you study hard, as I know you will, you'll get your degree or what-so-ever you call it, and a teacher'll be nothing to you! Still, though, I did want somebody to pass my tools on to. We can't get everything we want in this world."

David, a slim pale youth, looked at his father with admiration. Mr Holt was in his early sixties, a very strong robust man who was only happy when he was working. David gazed hard at his father, committing him to memory, as the thought of going away made him feel homesick in advance. Yet what could he do? He had always tried to please, and being very perservering, had pleased everyone at school and home by passing every possible exam devised by officialdom to torment the young. He had passed the eleven plus, six "O" Levels and five "A" Levels. Sometimes he wondered where it would end. What came after university? Ah well, somebody was sure to tell him. He felt very flattered at the moment, as his father was drinking with him as one man to another. Hitherto, all David's drinking had been very clandestine. He would always remember this day, as his father's frank brown eyes looked him up and down with such hearty approval. Mr Holt's eyes gave him a striking, distinguished look, a look that was further enhanced by his silvered hair and suntanned appearance. The sun tan was acquired by many hours' outdoor labour, building garden sheds, poultry runs, pigeon lofts and even benches and tables for his friends and acquaintances, in his spare time and sometimes free of charge. Sad to say Mr Holt could no longer work as a carpenter, and now drove a van for his regular living. As an all-round carpenter of the old slow-but-steady school of perfectionists, he had found himself superseded by the new breed of specialists, whose apprenticeships trained them to be mere cogs in machines —turners, fitters and so forth—who could only perform one part of a job. "Conveyor belt carpentry" Mr Holt called it, but nevertheless, the new breed were greatly favoured by the Unions, who ensured their high pay as long as they did not step out of line, and do a fitter's job if they were a turner. As for Mr Holt's conception of a carpenter, in Union ideology it did not exist, and he could be an errand boy in a workshop or seek employment outside the trade. If only the Holts had known it, the smart set in the South would have delighted in the family talent, and set them all to work imitating antique furniture. Such a sophisticated world, however, would not have suited Mr Holt at all, for though he had scoffed good naturedly at his late wife's addiction to hymn-singing and praying, he had a somewhat strictly puritan sense of morality. When perplexed, he consulted the Bible as if an almanac, and was fond of stating, almost defiantly, that Jesus Christ and Karl Marx were the greatest men who ever lived. As far as David knew, his father had never read Karl Marx, and though Mr Holt's views were far to the right of the Tories, he considered himself a Liberal. David himself had never tried to understand politics, and his main interests were train spotting, football and pop music.

" A penny for your thoughts, son! " shouted Mr Holt, who seldom spoke quietly.

" I just wondered, Dad, " blurted out David in sudden excitement, " if it wouldn't be better for me to chuck it all and become a carpenter! "

Mr Holt was amazed and delighted, and slapped David buoyantly across the shoulder blades.

" Good for you! Good for you! " he beamed. " I'll tell them at the depot what you said! You're a chip off the old block, that you are! Mind you, I won't hear of it. What! Give up a chance like this to get a proper education and meet and talk to people I would never dream of meeting! Aye, for that's what you'll do, you know— meet all these young gentlemen, the sons of the nobility, most like. Now that was what I wanted to warn you about. These young scholars, you see, you may find them toffee-nosed and stand-offish, at first, but don't let that put you off. There'll be plenty of football, and other sports too, I'll reckon, like rowing and cricket and so on. You might even find yourself a young lady. But listen carefully. I know these young gentlemen—well, that is, I've heard tales—and they can be very wild. Davey-lad, I don't want you to feel you have to prove yourself to them by playing the muggins and getting expelled. Drink and smoke in reason, and even have a little flutter on a horse if you have to, but none of this staying up all night at cards or climbing up steeples in the dark. The government can't give you another grant if you lose that one, and in the same way, the Lord can't give you another life. I won't be there to take my belt to you, you understand! "

" Yes Dad, " David smiled. "The belt" had been a

kind of comic bogey man figure in his life once, often mentioned but very rarely used. He had never heard it spoken of since he had put on his first pair of long trousers, until now, as a joke.

Refusing his father's suggestion that he look up his friends to say goodbye, David went up to his bedroom to pack. He was leaving to catch the train the next morning and his new home would be a room in the residency hall of a brand new Midland university, which only began its working life on the very same day. His subject was Economics, for the reason that he and his former economics teacher had taken a great liking to each other. He folded his belongings and crammed them into the old brown suitcase with his father's initials on it. Goodbye childhood, goodbye all those happy days! If only he didn't have to go!

Yet next day, after dreaming of his mother, he cheered up slightly, for as his father saw him up the road, they passed a chimney sweep. The sweep plodded dourly along, black from head to foot, with little red bloodshot eyes that peered rather nastily from the surrounding soot-filled wrinkles of his face. On his back he carried his brush Indian papoose style, poking out of a bag like a long-necked fuzzy wuzzy.

" Aha! " shouted Mr Holt. " That's a sign of luck! Now you should be all right, Davey-boy! "

To David's suprise and disappointment, the university was many miles away from the town it was named after, and with many others, all bewildered and grumbling, he had to wait twenty minutes for the country bus. The long-suffering conductor put them all off in the midst of some really beautiful countryside, so everyone was most annoyed, as they had expected to be surrounded on every side by pubs, coffee bars, restaurants, record shops and discothèque-clubs. Surely all their studying could not be in vain? Oh well, nothing for it but to follow the large signposts down the twisting lane and hope for the best.

David looked wonderingly at his fellow students, and swiftly gathered that his father was wrong in supposing that they would be the sons of earls. Everyone seemed to be from a grammar school the same as himself. He had been for his interview before, but this had been at the old premises in the town, a Technical College that had been doing duty as a university pending the Grand Opening. The others all seemed to have been interviewed there as well, which is why nobody now knew quite what to expect. There were hardly any girls among them, David noticed regretfully. He did not know it, but this was because the university curriculum paid scant attention to the Arts and Social Sciences, so beloved by the fair sex. In fact, the university was supposed to be geared for industry, and had a large endowment from both a local car factory and the Trades Union Congress. The most important question that each prospective candidate was asked was "Father's Occupation". If the occupation could be classified as "working class", you were in. Social engineering had become a favourite game among educationalists, and in this case the idea was partly to jolt up the intelligence level of trade union officials and partly to supply industry with executives and managers who were sympathetic to the working man. These aforesaid educationalists would have been very surprised to hear the views of Mr Holt on the Unions, which he often roundly declared to be " the curse of the working man. "

" What right, " Mr Holt would go on to anyone who would listen, " has one man, elected unopposed 'cos it's lunch hour, to stand up and talk gobbledegook in the name of thousands? No one else, save the few, can understand what he's on about, so why should they be called 'blacklegs' if they disobey him? Yet the high-ups, who think all working men are like him, are made to hate the workers who they think are all reds, so there you are! The politicians, too, are hoodwinked and reckon everyone wants more socialism! Socialism, fiddlesticks! I remember my Dad and his mates grumbled more than anyone when that Lloyd George brought in the National Insurance . . ."

If only Mr Holt had been able to keep abreast of modern trends, he would have gratefully accepted David's offer to be a carpenter. Yet, to understand these trends, he would have to be a far less likeable person than he actually was.

Meanwhile, David, in his sixth former's grey suit, was merely one grey-suited youth among scores. Not one arty person could be seen, although some of the scholars laughed and shouted rather coarsely to hide their timidity. At last they reached a large, white, ultra-modern building standing by a large newly-planted lawn with a pond and a fountain in the centre. This edifice, which looked a bit like a multi-storey car park, was in fact a combination of lecture halls and administrative offices. Bewildered, the newcomers were shepherded into the corridors by a very important looking person—in fact, the porter. Inside there was a count of heads and some official shilly-shallying, and then they were sent off on yet another Grand Trek across the countryside, this time to the Residential and Social Quarters, where the Vice Chancellor awaited them. Each day more students were arriving, virtually all bemused youngsters from non-academic homes, and the academic term proper would not start for another four days.

Despite feeling rather insecure and nervous, David now began to perk up a little, for the countryside really was *very* pretty. A tarmac path, flanked by lamp posts, curved down a hill cutting a swathe through the rich brown of the ploughed fields, and finally plunging into the depths of a most gorgeous oak wood, like a scene of old Merrie Englande. All around, woods and fields merged from green to misty blue as they faded into the September horizon. Inside the woods, David paused, allowing thirty other students to overtake, as he admired the shadowy depths of mossy trunks and sprouting bracken. He was to grow to love this walk, especially at night, when he was returning from an evening in the town's pubs. Then the lamp-posts lit up the woods as if by searchlight, and David could enjoy the illusion of being some wild woodland creature, able to see in the dark as he prowled on his nocturnal errands. Bounded by a frame of darkness, the illuminated trees and under-growth seemed crystal clear, more so than by sunlight, and David would gaze at these living pictures, hoping to glimpse a spot-lit view of the owls and foxes whose cries echoed from deeper within the strip of forest.

On this particular day, David emerged from the trees

to see, on the other side, a world of chaos in the glaring sun. Acres and acres of rich arable land was being churned up by bulldozers, and uprooted hedges and electrically sawn-down oak trees lay there in a shambles of banked-up earth. This was to be a "university city complex", or student community of never-ending Halls of Residence and various social centres.

The Halls and Social Centre already erected seemed extensive enough, both being huge white tiled buildings looking like very modern factories, with row upon row of large windows. Both were big, but the Halls were bigger and were actually a series of eight similar blocks, with narrow passageways between each one. A terrace of steps, lawns and flowers separated the Halls from the Centre, and a smiling lecturer (supposed by most to be a porter) ushered them all into the latter. Clearly, the Powers That Be had spent a king's ransom of mostly public money to make the young scholars comfortable.

Inside, almost half the ground floor of the Centre was taken up by an enormous room full of low tables and modernistic seats made of rubber and curving chrome metal. These, and the strip lighting, plus the unreal impersonal atmosphere, were to later earn the room the title of "The Airport Lounge". On this occasion, some of the chairs and tables were arranged in a semi-circle, in front of which the Vice Chancellor sat, with a few of his staff at either side. When the students were all seated, he arose and welcomed them and then launched into a long speech about the purpose of the new university and the challenges it offered and so on and so forth.

One by one, the students slipped into the coma that is the normal response to an uninterrupted speech. David

saw the Vice Chancellor's mouth opening and shutting,
and heard the rise and fall of tone, but in his mind he was
studying the Vice Chancellor and wondering what sort
of person he really was. He seemed a fussy, pompous
man in his grey suit, stout paunch and rather fierce
spectacles.

What he was actually saying at that moment was this:
". . . The day, we now recognise, is long past when
young men and women in their teens were regarded as
children, to be protected from the ill-effects of Society.
We are confident that the New Adults of your
generation, in spite of it being, for many of you, your
first time away from home, can conduct yourselves with
responsibility and organise your own affairs without any
help from us—er—old fogies on the staff—ha, ha! In
consequence of this realisation, for your part, we entrust
you absolutely with the running, organisation and care
of this entire portion of the—er—campus, the part of
the university that is, as I may put it, For Students Only.
Needless to say, this means that we, all of us, on the staff,
are fully aware that this shift of emphasis upon
responsibility from staff to student will meet with
criticism. It is up to you all, for the sake of yourselves and
of your university to prove the critics wrong. It is not
an abdication of responsibility, nor a betrayal of your
parents, but rather an experiment in student self-help
that we are sure will be met with an appreciative response
on your parts. Needless to say, you will have your
problems, and the man you will take them to is right by
my side—Mr Finch, our Welfare Officer. Never be
afraid to seek his advice at any time, at Room 47b in the
Administrative Building, on the third floor. This is our

only concession to the outmoded concept of a university's staff as being 'in loco parentis' . . ."

The boy on David's left woke up with a start.

" What was that about locos? " he enquired under his breath. " I'm a loco spotter myself. "

" It's not that sort of loco! " said David, smiling. " He was quoting French or something. I'm a spotter too; where-abouts are you from, then? "

" London, but I've been going to boarding school in Kent. "

The two boys had a whispered conversation about railway yards that they knew. David regretted the passing of steam, but his new friend, Edward, was full of enthusiasm for the diesel trains of the Midlands and North—trains that bridge the gap between railway and bus travel, with their rows of upright seats and bells that ring when entering and leaving a station. By the time that the Vice Chancellor and his merry men had departed, leaving the students in unrealised possession, David and Edward had mentally vowed to stick together as they explored their strange world.

Edward was a boy of unusual appearance, with short curly hair, large tortoiseshell-framed spectacles and very intense bright eyes with a slight squint. He was very exciteable, and spoke in rapid squeaks, nodding his head furiously and flapping his hands. No one meeting him for the first time would ever suppose him to be fifteen years old, let alone eighteen, but nobody could help but be touched by his eager frisking manners. At his last school, the other boys had believed him to be mad, and teased him good naturedly in consequence, but thanks to an almost photographic memory, he excelled them all at passing exams. He came from a very poor and scatter-brained family, and like David, he had lost his mother when quite young. When Edward was eleven years old, his father was arrested and imprisoned for forcing Edward's sister, who was in her last year at school, into an incestuous relationship. This left the girl somewhat feeble minded, and left the Welfare Workers with a problem—what to do with Edward? The boy had already passed the eleven-plus scholarship, and so it was decided to place him in a State-run boarding school, deep in the country. The school, a magnificent white mansion, set in parkland among cedars, rhododendrons and sweeping lawns, had once been the stately home of an earl, who had been forced by death duties to sell out. This displaced nobleman was still patron of the church and owner of the village, but now he lived in a nearby bungalow, his family portraits laid up in the village hall as a present to his tenants, who hung them up on fêtes and feast days. His father's ghost, and the ghost of his favourite dog, were supposed to haunt the terrace facing the French windows, but Edward had never seen them. In fact, Edward had felt very lost, as the staff were remote and uncaring, and many of the boys were bullies. All the pupils were supposed to be bright, but from "problem families", and they were supposed to be receiving a simulated public school education. Edward's school was intended as a rehearsal for the day when Eton and Harrow would be inundated with "problem" pupils from broken homes, as there had once been a fleeting fashion for such a notion. In consequence of this now defunct fashion, boys who were already insecure were snatched away from every familiar surrounding,

and were seriously expected to grow up into English
gentlemen, a breed of being of whose very existence they
were totally unaware. Edward, therefore, had emerged
from a world of total confusion, especially as each
holiday saw him transplanted from the dormitory and
rugger pitch to the junk-filled spare room of his uncle,
a scrap metal dealer in Walworth. If the boy was a little
strange, it was not to be wondered at.

" Are you trying for the B.Sc. Economics the same as
me? " he now asked David.

" Yes, that's right; let's have a look round now, shall
we? "

" Yes, okay. It's only three years to go, and then we
can leave. I've been dying to leave school, 'cos it's my
ambition to be a train driver, but there's always more
exams to pass. "

In amazement, David and Edward strolled around, up
and down stairs, to explore their palatial domain. Could
all this really be theirs, in absolute freedom, to enjoy
whenever they felt like it? As well as the lounge, there
was a sports room with facilities for table football and
table tennis, a dining room, a television lounge, rows of
machines that vended hot drinks, sweets and cigarettes,
and an actual pub! This in the afternoons sold soft
drinks, and was staffed by young people who looked
like students but were not. Such young people, many of
them dissatisfied former office workers, were unable to
resist the mystique of a university, and had been prompt
to apply for jobs no matter how menial. Some served
meals, others held white collar posts, and some sold
magazines and newspapers from a stall set up in the
Airport Lounge. As they were older than the students,

and had arrived first, they could not help feeling superior. Not that it would be hard to feel superior to the flocks of lost sheep dazedly wandering around their pastures new, without a shepherd for the first time in their lives. In other words, there were No Grown Ups, and the far from rebellious students did not quite know what to do with themselves. Someone turned the television on, others ordered drinks, but most of them collected their keys from the office and went to look at their sleeping quarters.

David and Edward compared rooms, and found little to choose between them. This is not surprising, for though the Halls of Residence contained nothing but bedsittingrooms, thousands of them, all in rows, floor upon floor, yet each room was exactly the same as the next. The man who had designed the ideal "student room" had been granted an award for his labours, and his plan had been adopted without variance. Every room contained a small bed, a wardrobe, washbasin, writing desk, fitted carpet, armchair and a low circular table, all scientifically packed. One wall was taken up by a large curtained window, on one of the other walls stood a notice warning about fire danger, and here and there bizarre modern standard lamps craned their extendable necks as if in enquiry. All quite suitable, yet rather overpowering by sheer force of numbers. Very soon, of course, every room began to take on the unmistakeable character of its owner, as personal effects were unpacked and put into place.

By the time David had unpacked, he felt quite exhausted, so he climbed into bed and spent an hour or so reading the treasured comic annuals he had brought from home. Then he switched off the bedside lamp and lay down feeling very alone and despondent. Soon he was asleep, to be awoken next morning by the clanging and banging of the cleaners in the corridor. Hurriedly washing and dressing, he ran out to see what was for breakfast. On his way, he passed the cleaners, a group of middle-aged pleasant-looking motherly women. Here he was faced with a dilemma—what was he supposed to say to them? An experienced man of the world would have said something like this:

" Good morning, nice day. "

David did not know this, and his emotions were similar to those of an inexperienced tipper in an unusually classy restaurant. Panic struck his breast as he saw yet another cleaner emerge from a boy's room— the students actually had servants, or at least bedmakers! This was something quite outside his ken, and he turned his head dumbly as he walked by, breaking into a slight sweat. A hurt silence seemed to assail his back. Although no one spoke of it, virtually none of the students felt at ease with the cleaners, and the most acknowledgment the latter received would be a shy nod or an embarrassed grunt. Consequently, if any visitor should actually *speak* to the poor cleaners, those hardworking ladies would be pathetically grateful.

After about a month, the students, David and Edward included, had settled down into a vague kind of routine. They would generally attend a lecture in the morning, and then moon around in the afternoon and evening, perhaps filling in time by writing an essay or attending yet another incomprehensible lecture. As the town was so far away, and buses were infrequent, the students mainly hung around the pub or the television lounge. On Thursday evenings they became very animated, as this was the time when "Top of the Pops" was broadcast. Young scholars could be seen running towards the lounge from every direction as seven-thirty approached, and the latecomers would have to sit on the floor. Edward took this programme very seriously, and tried to make a graph to show the popularity of the new hit songs among the students who read Economics.

David, however, was a bit distracted by difficulties with his chosen subject. Lecturers would hurry into their halls, fix their gaze upon the wall above the students' heads, rattle off some incomprehensible jargon in a cold, impersonal manner, and then hurry out. Plainly they regarded the actual teaching as the one annoying drawback to an otherwise splendidly cushy job. Some would dash off notes on the blackboard for the students to copy, but most of them expected notes to be made from their hastily delivered monologues. As for original ideas and personal opinions, these were strictly taboo, and any student who did not learn to build his essays from bricks of parrot-learned phrases would find a red line swept right across his work. It was all right for Edward, David thought glumly, as he had a most uncanny memory, and knew in exactly what order to place all the long words. But he would never be able to master this frightful subject. At school, the Economics seemed to be about the concrete use of money, and his teacher had been patient and kindly. But here it was all theory, taking place in an unreal limbo of endless chunks of long-windedness. He could learn these chunks by heart, but he and his fellows found it hard to place them in the arrangements that their lecturers required. Most of these lecturers were only a few years older than their audiences, and led a very gay life of parties, pub crawls and sports cars, from which all but some of the girl students were excluded.

However, David's lecturer in Economic History was middle-aged, and though a rather drab, dour personage, he took some interest in his classes. He had not been a card-bearing Communist since the 'thirties, but his ideas were frozen in the attitudes of his youth. Painstakingly he would explain to his charges about how Capitalism evolves by itself and finally dies, and blandly the students would find out what he wanted and try to give it to him.

Not only the ideals of the students were becoming tarnished, but the very gleaming modernity of their university was suffering a similar fate. The white tiles which gave the Halls of Residence their distinctive appearance had now begun to fall off, leaving unsightly grey square patches here and there. Not only this, but as they usually fell from a great height, whistling through the air and then exploding into fragments on the concrete path below, they represented a danger to life and limb. As if from nowhere, notices appeared one morning telling everyone to " Beware of Falling Tiles. " A rumour went about that the university was built cheaply by the Chancellor's brother-in-law, supposedly an unscrupulous local builder.

However, the one unspoken problem that bewildered the students, was what to think about in their ample spare time. Up till now, their minds were trained to look ahead to the next examination, but now the only serious exam would be their finals in three years' time. If a lecturer or any adult had organised a sports' club, they would have been delighted, but as it was left to them, nothing was done, as no one liked to take the initiative. A kind of mental vacuum prevailed, as if of a number of souls released into an empty Heaven with no God or even any archangels to reassure them that it was perfectly all right. The Oxbridge conception of a university as a place to gain culture did not apply here, as, for these scholarship children, reading was what you did to pass exams, nothing to do with the pleasures of literature.

David read and re-read his comic books however, and then finally, without really realising it, he began to draw comic pictures of dragons and moon monsters. One of these, his favourite, he coloured in crayons and then wrote below in his sprawling handwriting: " The Martian Seven Legged Green and Red Spotted Rock Borer. Especially fond of Hamadryads. "

Full of impish glee, he ran across to the Social Centre and pinned his brainchild on an austere notice board. He then watched a cowboy film on television for an hour, and on his way out, he noticed a crowd of twenty or more gathered around his picture in hilarious excitement. Modestly he joined them, but after a moment he could not contain himself, and blurted out that he was the artist.

" How did you learn to draw so good? " asked one tall boy.

" Oh well, I just looked at the pictures in the comic books I've brought from home. "

" Cor, did your parents allow you to read *comics*? "

gasped this boy, whose home was strict. To David's surprise, many of the students had never heard of the *Hotspur* or even of the *Dandy* and *Beano*! Thus began happy days for David, as his room became a salon, with boys almost queuing to knock on his door and shyly ask permission to come in and read his annuals. Proudly he would sit there, wishing his Dad could see him, as students sat on his bed, floor and table, choking and rocking with laughter over the exploits of "Desperate Dan", "Keyhole Kate" and "Biffo the Bear"—to say nothing of "Lord Snooty and his Pals".

Alas, how fickle is popularity! David's true glory as a sponsor of the Arts only lasted for four weeks, and then another boy began to give readings in the lounge from his own copies of *Winnie the Pooh* and *The House at Pooh Corner*.

For most of the boys, this was their first introduction to real literature, read for its own sake. Its effect was electrifying, and a Pooh cult swept the university, even causing indulgent comment from some of the less slow-witted lecturers. If these boys had read A. A. Milne's delightful stories at an earlier age, as the author had intended, their joy in literary humour and plot might have led them on to a fuller appreciation of our island's idyllic classic fiction. As it was, they were almost unbalanced in ecstasy, much as young people from Godless homes succumb hysterically to the stirring messages of fundamentalist preachers. Chalk pictures of Winnie the Pooh, Kanga, Tigger, Piglet and Rabbit appeared on every available blackboard and paving stone, many of these being drawn by David himself. Edward, too, was hard hit by the craze and with great trouble he made an Eeyore's tail out of cloth and hung it on his door as if it was Owl's bell-pull. (Those in perplexity, consult your local children's library.)

This fashion lasted a full six weeks, and never entirely died out, as some of the diehards formed a "Pooh Society". David now felt he was getting into the swing of university life, which apparently consisted of endless highly enjoyable fashions. As yet, the students were still sixth form in mentality, but sad to say, the innocuous "Pooh Society" was the beginning of the end. For from that day on, Societies of every kind sprang up like toadstools, with a committee that attracted the more pushy and organisation-minded of the boys.

Hence a rather shrill note appeared for the first time in the university. Rival heads of committees touted for members in a rather rude way, and the standard of manners and politeness began to slip.

Following in the footsteps of Winnie the Pooh, the next preoccupation proved to be Folk Music. One or two boys had always sat in corners, strumming guitars and rather self-consciously inviting anyone who came near to join in some unrecognisable chorus, but now this pastime had been taken over by a Society, and became immensely serious. Less music was played, and instead factions formed who all angrily debated on what was True Folk Music. Soon, virtually *no* music was played, perhaps fortunately, and offshoot Societies appeared, all arguing that their case presented the true gospel. Some maintained that after a certain date (though no two people could agree when) no folk music was capable of being produced. Others insisted that any new song was a folk song if it fitted a certain criterion, though no one could agree what. All the factions claimed that folk music was the Voice of the Oppressed, but no one could agree who the oppressed were. A tense, smouldering atmosphere began to be built up.

David, who did not enjoy folk music in the least, now felt rather aimless and fed-up. He associated Folk Music with schoolmasters, and considered it the Voice of the Book Learned, the people who made exams. He supposed it was all right, but why a song was superior for having been composed before the copyright laws were passed, he could not see. Edward, too, was uninterested in the new vogue, especially as its devotees were turning their noses up at his favourite pop stars, claiming them to be "commercial". Recently, David had had an essay returned with a red line across it, so he felt he was being nagged at from every side. Supposing David's laboured, anguished and sweated-over errors to be due to an airy carelessness, the lecturer had written in the margin—" Do not abuse your privilege. Remember what you are here for. "

Dully, David gazed at this insulting message, until he flushed with righteous anger. Hang it all, what *was* he there for? No one had told him, he simply knew that passing exams led to university. What the university was there for, and what he was doing in it, were questions that had never before occurred to him. Now they did so, very forcibly. Why had mere examinations, consisting of words and paper, the Gestapo-like power to drag him away from home and family and chosen career, and shut him up miles from anywhere in a benevolent but apparently useless institution? He had seldom found time as the "brains of the family" to learn much about carpentry, but he liked the feel of wood. Whereas, as the subject was now taught, he hated the feel of Economics, and he hadn't the least idea of what an Economist did to earn his bread. Vaguely, he felt that whatever it was, it wasn't honest, but probably consisted in pretending to some gullible civil servant or businessman that you could understand long words and predict the future.

In coming to this instinctive conclusion, David had hit the nail on the head, and proved once more the superiority of common sense over mere Reason. Like many dissatisfied students, he felt a glimmering of understanding that the academic world had been swamped by pseudo-sciences; perverted doctrines that led to pseudo-useful careers of bureaucratic sham and cynical mockery. Unlike the run-of-the-mill disillusioned student, he did not suppose that he knew how to handle the situation, but instead sought the advice and company of Edward.

(The Welfare Officer, supposedly in charge of all student problems, had never had a visitor since the term began. Pathetically, he sat in his tiny room, 47b, and did crossword puzzles, glancing yearningly at the doorknob from time to time, hoping against hope that one day he would have a chance to be useful.)

Edward gave his friend a look of mute despair, as he had been trapped by a folk music person who was trying to get him to fill in a typed out membership form.

" I'm sick of Economics, " David said wearily. " I'll never understand it. "

" It's not for understanding, it's for learning, " Edward replied. " It doesn't worry me, 'cos I'm going to be a train driver, and they don't really need it, though of course it's an advantage. "

The folk music person, who sported a pair of mutton chop side-whiskers, gave a start at this.

" You can't just leave here and be a train driver! " he protested. " It's not right to waste all that training. "

" But what are we being trained *for*? " persisted David.

" Oh, I don't know. Careers in industry, I think— executives and that. "

" Is there any appeal, do you know? " asked David. " I can't really understand politics, but you'd think that we could choose our own careers. After all, what do I know about industry—or care, for that matter? It'd be different if we could leave school and go into industry learning it as we went along, but what will they teach me here about executives? They don't even come into the course I'm doing, as far as I can see. "

" No, no, you don't understand at all, " protested the whiskered one. " All we do here is get degrees, like. It's the degree that's the thing, that's what we're being trained for. The employer picks us out by the quality of our degrees, and then *he* trains us for the job, on executive courses and that. That way, it's instead of the bad old days of leaving school for an apprenticeship and starting work in your teens—now we can stay on at university for ever, getting grants, and not start work till we're getting on for thirty. It's better, obviously. "

" Well, " considered David, " it's all right I suppose, but it seems too compulsory. Also, employers can't be that bright to fall for it. You'd think they'd pick a bloke for what he knew of the job, not for the letters after his name. No wonder craftsmanship is dying out, just like my Dad said. I'd sooner be an apprentice than be idle half the time. . . "

Both boys looked at him in amazement. Of course, in one sense, all the students were State apprentices, with all the attendant wastage and folly that goes with a government function that could better be done by shrewd private enterprise. Few of the scholars were aware of art and high society, especially as there was no one on the staff to tell them, and in an earlier age they would all have been out at work learning a trade or perhaps even a profession. As it was, modern businessmen, cushioned by State aid and bemused by State advice as never before, might well take many of them on and perhaps even help them to overcome their wasted years spent recuperating from a surfeit of examinations. But what of the scholar who looks on the university as a career in itself? David, Edward and many of the others had never been consulted about a career at all, as actual work was supposed to be demeaning compared with university life. The whole thing didn't seem to make sense, now that David was actually in a university, and he felt a sense of futility that would have sent many a student to the barricades. Fortunately, politics had not yet appeared at this particular university.

" Since I left the original Folk Music Society, " Edward's friend rambled on, " I have formed a Blues Society to compete with the Ethnic Traditionalists and the Post Dylan Modernists. The idea of this came to me 'cos I noticed that the bloke next door to me had all these blues records. We'll play them at our meetings, see, and then we can make speeches about them and so on.

We can all buy bottled beer, and it should be great. Are you coming tonight, Edward? "

" Yeh, I s'pose so, " was the reply, and the Organisation Man beetled off.

" I'm feeling utterly cheesed off, " David confessed. " Since all these Societies sprang up, I've had nothing to do, and I don't like meetings and committees. I feel a bit lost with no grown ups about at all. You'd think they'd come over here once in a while and see how we were getting on. "

" You're daft, " said Edward. " There's one in here now—that bloke playing table tennis. He takes mathematics and he comes from Israel. "

David cast an eye over the lecturer, a young man in his early twenties wearing shorts, spectacles and a very large Adam's apple. He was hopping about excitedly and looking rather comical, so David had to eat his words. What he really wanted, without being quite conscious of it, was someone to respect.

Some weeks later, David found himself praying for the end of term and the sanity of his humble home. The whole university had gone blues crazy, and young men in casual clothes, despite the approach of winter, lurched about the place singing things like "Oowee lawdy mama" to themselves. David could not stand it, but fortunately it was only a few days now until term's end. Edward, to his own surprise, had succumbed completely to the blues mania, and chattered admiringly of this singer who had committed two murders, that one who had been killed with an ice pick, or been poisoned by a girlfriend or who was doing time for manslaughter.

" You can't go about slaughtering men, " David

reasoned with his friend. " They seem a right old lot, these blues singers. Let alone their croaky voices, they've got no sense of romance like an ordinary singer has. They go from one woman to another, treating them all like dirt, and then moaning that the woman's leaving them. Either that or they're planning to leave *her*, or kill her or something. Why don't they get married and get steady jobs? "

" You don't understand at all! " wailed the obsessed Edward, in his agitation sounding almost like one of his own idols. " When they're singing about a woman, what they *really* mean is that the slums are too overcrowded, the police carry guns and use them, the sharecropper system is wrong, that men are unjustly sentenced for crimes they did not do, and the whole American system, with its wars and tear gas and Ku Klux Klans and ill-treated Red Indians, must be destroyed! That's what they *really* mean. Anyway, the women aren't much good, as they keep going to church, and don't like the men playing blues 'cos they think it's of the devil. Really, it's the music of an oppressed, unhappy people, forced to rob, cheat, steal and kill. It must be glorious being an American Negro, on your own against the whole world, like a noble outlaw! If only I could be one, or get to know them—wouldn't it be great? "

" I suppose so, " said David resignedly. It seemed a shame to destroy America, despite that country's faults, but he couldn't really take Edward's new ideas seriously. A song was only a song, after all.

David enjoyed a quiet Christmas at home with his father, brother and Bible-reading Auntie, and during the holidays he received two letters from Edward. The latter had joined several London blues clubs, where students from all over the place plunked guitars and tried to imagine themselves as Negroes on the Mississippi Delta. He had enjoyed himself immensely, and his letters left David wondering what crazes would help to occupy their time in the following term. Personally, he was going back to train spotting.

As the holidays neared their end, David began to fret slightly, for he had an essay to complete and there were some books he was supposed to read. One frosty day, he was stepping gingerly along a slippery brick-paved street towards his house with some library books under his arm. Looking up, he met the dreamy gaze of the Methodist minister, and before he had time to escape, that worthy had fallen into step with him and started a conversation. Poor David felt embarrassed, for neither he nor his father bothered to go to chapel any more.

The minister was tall and boney, with white hair and pale cloudy blue eyes. When a young man he had led a happy life as a seaman, and for the last thirty years he had been even happier repenting of it. He was a mild, serene person and he beamed at David and looked at his books with great respect.

"You young people are so fortunate with your education," the minister rhapsodised.

David was glad he thought so.

"Yes, especially as you are studying Economics," the good minister pursued. "Why, a knowledge of Economics is almost, I say 'almost', as valuable as a knowledge of the Bible in pointing out to us our Father's wisdom. By seeing how commerce depends upon the high and the lowly alike, we see that all men are equal before God. The man who makes the smallest part of a machine is just as vital to the completed task as the man who owns the factory. All men depend on one another, and who is to say that one is more important than another? The work we do, as your teachers will have explained, is like the pieces of a jigsaw puzzle. We need the street sweeper as much as the financier, and of course the other way about, so as to create a complete harmony in accordance to the wishes of our Heavenly Father. I know this is old hat to someone as lucky as you, and if I had not left school at fourteen, I would have realised it sooner. But there—you don't want to hear the ramblings of an old man, I'm sure. Tell me something about your studies—I'm sure you must find it fascinating."

David mumbled something, and then made his getaway. As he did so, he wondered what would happen if he put the minister's views into his essay. He couldn't very well be flogged, but he might be expelled. Wherever would his history lecturer fit in the minister's (or God's) scheme of things? As the lecturer in question did not *believe* in God, perhaps he was exempt from usefulness, or possibly he was a luxury that the country could afford. David could not decide about God. If there was a God, the whole world would then seem to make sense, even to someone as stupid as he felt himself to be. But surely that answer was too simple, and really the long words, if they could only be understood instead of learned by heart, explained everything that there was to know.

That evening he began to tussle with the long words, with his father looking on admiringly. As the weather was cold, Mr Holt had taken his woodwork indoors. Had his wife been alive, she would have been horrified to see it, for he had ingeniously fastened one end of a plank onto the edge of the front room table with a vice, and the other end was jammed against the bannisters in the hall. He had put newspapers on the floor and was now cheerfully planing away, with intriguingly curly twirls of wood shavings falling everywhere. Even this routine task gave him great pleasure, and his dark eyes shone boldly as he chatted away to his studious second-born who was crouched in an easy chair with his books.

David felt soothed by the rasp of the plane as it took his mind off the appalling text books he was staring at.

"What've you got to write, son?" called out Mr Holt carelessly.

"An essay on the causes of the Second World War."

"Ah well, you've come to the right bloke now. It was only one cause—you can put this—'The cause of the Second World War was short, 'e 'ad a black moustache, 'e made speeches'."

"Don't be silly, Dad, they want an economical cause. Economics isn't about people, our lecturers say, it's about forces."

Mr Holt conceded this as he supposed his son knew best, whatever he was talking about. The only forces Mr Holt knew anything about were the Armed Forces, in which he had served honourably during the last war, reaching the rank of sergeant. Naturally his views would be of no help to his son.

"You've got to put what the lecturers like or you don't get good results," explained David, who did not like to see his father look small. "You've got to run down someone called Adam Smith like mad, and keep praising Karl Marx. "

" Ah, that's what I've always said. You can't beat these wise old Jews, not when it comes down to brass tacks, like. When I was a lad, I used to visit my uncle in Leeds, and I used to see all these old Jewish wise men there—men with grey beards, black 'ats and such kind interesting looking faces, all crinkles and little brown eyes. Like olden day wizards they seemed to me then, always clutching books writ in some foreign tongue— you could see they were learned. People go on at Jews sometimes, but that's only jealousy. Never, never in my dreams then did I think I'd grow up to 'ave a son at university, who could understand all the knowledge these old Jews had. You couldn't do better than keep at your studies. Why, when I was young, if someone round 'ere was good at book learning, they'd count 'im lucky if 'e was a clerk or summat. That just shows 'ow things 'ave changed. "

David blushed and felt very guilty of the con-trick he had somehow been forced into playing on his father.

" I'm not as bright as you think, Dad, " he confessed honestly. " Were the German workers poor, and did Hitler promise higher wages, do you know? "

" Can't say I do, son. Sounds likely though, doesn't it? It just shows what I've always said—if you mess about with wages you mess everything up. Like these trade union people—they force wages up 'cos they don't realise that guv'nors are human. They seem to think that all guv'nors are in the wrong, and that they're sitting on huge bags of gold, like. Well, I know better, 'cos my Dad 'ad 'is own workshop an' hired men, and the facts are these—if 'e'd 'ave paid 'is men more than 'e could afford, 'e'd 'ave 'ad to charge 'is customers more, to make it up. Now a man might, thanks to 'is union, get higher wages, but what then? 'Is wife'll want more 'ousekeeping, that's what, 'cos things in the shops'll go up. My Dad always used to tell 'is men, before 'e hired them, what 'e could pay, and if they didn't like it they needn't work for 'im. That's 'ow it was then, but what with unions and taxes, the business couldn't go on, an' by the time I was grown, 'e was jobbing around 'ere and there. Well, I'm sorry son—I mustn't keep talking when you're trying to study. I can't help you much, 'cos I've never understood Economics or book talk or suchlike. I'll get on with the work I *do* know, and leave you in peace."

So saying, Mr Holt bent to his work once more, swishing the plane to and fro with an energy that reminded David of the way his mother had stood in the same spot doing the ironing. Now Mr Holt took most of the washing to the launderette in the town's new and ugly concrete precinct. Absently, Mr Holt began to whistle, but after a while he went out after paraffin, and David managed to muddle his way through his essay.

When the Easter term began, David decided to be adventurous and hitch-hike down. At the edge of the town he managed to talk his way into a coach that was taking a load of jovial miners on an outing. He put two shillings in the bag they passed around, and had a long and pleasurable ride, surrounded by brawny men all singing "The Blaydon Races", "Yellow Submarine" and sundry football songs that were really parodies of Methodist hymns.

Arriving at the university some hours after most of the others, David found the latest craze to be well under way, and he found also that his fraternising with coal miners gave him an honourable position in the hierarchy of the new cult.

He discovered Edward, who now looked very arty and effete, in conversation with a big hefty fellow of twenty-five or so—one of the few so-called "mature students".

" Have a nice holiday? " David enquired.

" Yeh, all righ' fanks, not so bad. Yourself? "

" Oh yes, I had quite a good time. I hitch-hiked back here, and a coachload of miners took me almost halfway—we had quite a laugh, all singing and drinking. You got a sore throat, by the way? "

" No, why? " replied Edward, still in a slurred voice, for the rage was now to be Working Class. Those whose parents were of humble stock were now the top dogs, and practised accents of unbelievable uncouthness, which would have astounded their parents. The imitation accents, soon to become genuine and a severe disability, were not the picturesque speech of genuine labourers, but rather almost a series of pre-human grunts, noises which said little for the grunter's opinion of the working man. Those students whose parents were white collar workers, either vaguely assumed that their parents were really working class after all, or else cast their minds back to distant grandfathers and great-grandfathers. If there was a workman somewhere in the family tree, you could relax, secure in your caste membership as any "working class" managing director, life peer or professor.

Meanwhile, Edward's friend gazed keenly at David, and then asked him if his father was a coal miner.

" No, but 'e's all righ', 'is ole man's a carpenter—chippie, tha' is, I mean, like, " put in Edward, anxious for David to make a good impression upon his influential friend.

" Ah well, as long as he's one of us, " said the President of the Students' Union magnanimously. This person had suddenly emerged from hiding, having spent the previous term in finding his feet, for the university was a far cry from the motor car factory where he had been a shop steward. He had been chosen as a working class scholar, capable of university education under a progressive scheme for inviting the non-academic citizen into academic realms. The management of the factory had seen this scheme as a Godsend for getting rid of their troublemakers, and in this new environment, Dick Scuddey (one of the Union Scuddeys) had shot up to be King in the brief moment it took him to elect himself Union President before most of the other students had returned. His father an eminent Trade Unionist, his position was now that of a duke's son in pre-war Oxford.

" Here you are, son " said this Scuddey patronisingly to David. " Your union card. "

" What's this? " asked David, looking at it in puzzlement. " I never applied to join, and I haven't paid anything. "

" Where's your solidarity, brother? " asked Dick Scuddey, but David, who thought he was being most unjustly accused of being fat, and who thought "brother" was said in sarcasm, said nothing and bit his lips in anger. The Trade Unionist therefore continued—" You are a member of the Union automatically, brother, and your dues are taken out of your government grant before it gets to you. It is up to you to take an interest in your union, as a member of the working class fighting against capitalism. Excuse me, I have other work to do. "

Clumping dourly, he departed, and his flat, mournful, monotonous voice which seemed to come from his nose, could be heard echoing around in the distance asking if everyone was sure they had their union cards.

" Great bloke, innee? " said Edward, whose new accent sat oddly on his frail and poetic exterior.

David did not relish this new preoccupation at all, but one who *did* was the Communist history lecturer, who may have regarded it as the increased class consciousness of the proletariat or something. His lectures even became slightly popular, and he kept coming out with phrases like " we of the articulate, politically motivated working class intelligentsia " which went down quite well. Dick Scuddey became a lecturers' pet as well as a students' idol, and some saw him as a future Labour Prime Minister. He was the first student to even think of entering the lecturers' quarters, which he did with a petition demanding a Union Building, envisaged as a mighty skyscraper. This demand was meekly agreed to " in the future " and the Man of Destiny successfully whipped up a surprising amount of emotional support from the students. Suddenly everyone realised that a Union Building was what they had always wanted and

indeed could not live without. Discussion raged into
the night, and many pamphlets were typed out and
duplicated.

One of these presented a pitiful portrait of the
university in ten years' time, complete with opera house,
theatre, art gallery but still no Union Building. No one
apparently saw it as incongruous that the writer should
imply that a Union Building be placed before any of the
fine arts. As it happened, the Union Building was now
actually on the agenda, while the idea of an art gallery
seemed laughable.

Edward left David to his comic books and frisked
excitedly around Dick Scuddey. Dick had such an air of
ponderous certainty that everyone was eager to kneel at
his feet and learn from him. The few girls appeared
from wherever they had been, and clustered around him.
Dick used to stroll onto the new building site and chat
to the labourers, while an awed crowd admired him
from the distance. The labourers, a cheerful bunch of
men, often wondered why someone should go such a
long way just to ask for a light, when the university
teemed with young smokers. On one red letter day in
the history lecturer's calendar, Dick introduced him to a
labourer and started a political discussion going. The
labourer's contribution was that only the re-introduction
of hanging would set the country on its feet again. If
an educated man had said as much, the lecturer would
have called him a "fascist", but as it was, he only
mumbled something and then trotted back to his room
to write an essay for *New Society* magazine on the
"deferential instinct" of the working man in aping the
ideas of the Conservatives. As for the labourer, who

supposed that all politicians were scoundrels, he in his turn looked on the lecturer with a gentle, amused pity as one of the weaker brethren.

One day Edward insisted that David come and listen to Dick Scuddey speaking informally to his faithful subjects in the airport lounge. They arrived to find the orator well under way.

" All us Scuddeys are a Union family, " he bragged in his stolid way. "All except the women that is—a worker's wife knows 'er place. My uncle was the first man to organise the packers in his home town—people who made up clothes into parcels. His brother said to 'im that packing was not a productive industry but merely service, and that therefore a packer was not a true productive proletarian but closer to a capitalist lackey. But my packer uncle would 'ave none of it. I well remember 'im in our little kitchen at home, kettle on the fire. There 'e sat, crouched forward on a wooden chair, hitting 'is 'ands on 'is knees while 'e thought. Finally 'e spoke, an' you could 'ave 'eard a pin drop. 'A packer produces a product,' 'e says, ' 'cos 'is product is a parcel. Therefore a packer is in a productive industry an' the product that 'e produces is a parcel, an' therefore it's a productive industry when parcels are packed or produced.'

" The very next day, 'e tells the packers this and they go out on strike. See, industry is only good if it's productive, obviously. The rest is decadent, 'cos it merely provides a service for people with money in their pockets, like in shops—that's the service industries. Production is what counts, 'cos where there's production, there's union strength. Where the worker is in contact with other classes, as with a shop assistant, there's union weakness. In Russia it's all production and no shops, and that's our goal. It's not so far off, not now that every working man is a socialist."

"My father is a Jehovah's Witness," somebody butted in irreverently. "He says it's wrong to vote as it's an attempt to alter Jehovah God's chosen destiny for us. Yet he's a working man—he does the drains for the council."

"As long as a man is a union member," Dick Scuddey spoke up severely, "'e's a socialist whether 'e wants to be or not. That's 'cos union money goes in part to the Labour Party, never mind what the opinions of the union members are. If it wasn't for compulsion, many working men would try an' escape from the unions and evade their class responsibility. The law's too vague— we want a definite legal penalty that'll make sure that everyone has to join a union. Then we can all have true Socialism."

At the last noble sentiment, Dick Scuddey's girlfriend beamed, her little eyes shining, and she snuggled up against his shoulder. David sat enthralled, not at the speech, which made his mind go blank, but because he had fallen for the girl who now claimed the speaker's attention. She was not a student, but a would-be student who worked in the canteen dishing out meals very inefficiently. He found her slight Glaswegian accent to be very appealing and sometimes spoke to her shyly of potatoes or cauliflower. Now here she was in his midst, almost accessible and yet belonging to Dick Scuddey. It was too bad!

Deserted by his friends, David built an obsession for

the girl, Helen Sheehan, and lay awake at night thinking about her.

Helen Sheehan had a very high opinion of herself and would not contemplate leaving school at fifteen and starting work as everyone else in her large family did as a matter of course. Her father, persuaded that she was brainy, supported her for five years, from fifteen to twenty, while she attended a technical college. She managed, during this time, to pass ten "O" Level examinations. By this time, she grew exasperated by the naïveties of her Glasgow Catholic family and applied for a clerical post in the new university. Failing that, she applied for every job going, just to be near students, and finally ended up in the canteen. Her hope was to catch a rich, fashionable and intellectual husband, and she thought Dick Scuddey would do, as she admired his sentiments about the working class. She herself was very proud of being working class, and ashamed of her family at the same time.

To an unbiased observer, Helen Sheehan seemed a very ordinary plump British maiden. Her skirt was very short, revealing huge legs of surprising beefiness, and her little eyes were hidden away among her well-fleshed pouting cheeks. Nevertheless, she was not round, but rather tall, and her skin somewhat of an olive colour. Her hair was long and brown and hung down over her shoulders in the prevailing manner of the day, and her mouth was small. When she opened it to speak, her voice emerged as an affected twitter, and she waved her hands about as if trying to seem clever and un-Glaswegian. To sum her up, she was sluggish and smug, and yet David adored her.

Because of this, the poor lad was torn between avoiding Dick Scuddey and associating with him, so he spent an unhappy term. Towards the end of it, he did manage to exchange a few words with Helen and told her what a pretty accent she had. She was not very pleased.

"*Foreign* languages are really my meteor," she said, throwing in a little "O" Level French as a sample. "I've done French *and* Russian for 'O' Level and my real career is to be a translator."

"Russian—struth!" said David greatly impressed. "Speak some Russian for me then. Say 'the wolves are chasing the sledge'."

"It's commercial Russian I've done," she replied loftily. "I can't do old fashioned words like 'wolves' or 'chasing' or 'sledge'."

"Oh, I see," said David, more impressed than ever.

During the summer holidays, David received an invitation from Edward to spend a fortnight with him in London, where he was now sharing a Notting Hill Gate flat with several blues fans. It all seemed very gay and bohemian, and David asked his father if he could go.

"Bless you, son, you don't have to ask me things like that any more," was the genial reply. "You're a young man now, you can do what you like. You go and enjoy yourself with your young gentleman friends, go on!"

So it was that after a bewildering day or two in the strange city, David found himself settled in with Edward and two other young men and did not like it at all.

For one thing, the flat was terribly squalid and messy.

It consisted of one huge room and a tiny kitchen, and David was startled to find that the others complacently expected him to sleep on the floor in his clothes.

"You should have brought a sleeping bag, man," one of them said. Edward was now quite acclimatised to this strange new life and grafted Americanisms onto his new accent in a bizarre manner that combined the blues ideology with the trade union jargon.

"I mean, like man, this guy comes up to me an' 'e says, 'e says 'cummere' like, you know," he would gabble with practised ease, while the others nodded approval. They had all progressed from blues to blues-based white surrealist music, sung by young men with the appearance of Rasputin going into a frenzy with wild insane eyes.

David found that the whole house and much of the street was given over to young people from mostly good homes who were acting out the fantasies they had culled from blues music, and lived as they imagined Negroes did on Chicago's South Side. They lived mostly on the dole except for occasional manual jobs and they also lived with one woman after another, with casual children being carried about from here to there, not knowing their own fathers. Edward's friends were not as bad as most, and they found him a large duffle coat to roll up in at night on the floor. Nevertheless, it occurred to him that perhaps the blues really *was* the devil's music, and he never again underestimated the power of a song. Music is a greater summons to arms than any theory ever expounded, and songs have caused the rise and fall of nations.

The girls who called in at the flat quite alarmed poor

David with their tangled hair and their foul language that seemed all the more shocking because its users were university educated. It seemed they relished nastiness, and David spent much of his time on his own in the South Kensington museums. Even the fragile Edward was surprisingly promiscuous, and David felt somehow that these people had an urge to change themselves utterly and be purged of all humanity.

After a night out in an intellectuals' coffee bar, David made up his mind to go home again the very next day. The coffee bar was neon lit, all in bluish-purple, so that ghastly purple faces loomed up here and there amidst the fish nets and surrealist decor. Modern jazz wailed away over the loudspeakers, with cold impersonal alto saxophones warbling up and down and round and round in eddies. David sat as in a trance, for the purple light and the detached music made him feel as if he was trapped in the unfeeling world of the living dead.

Little did the self-conscious inventors of modern jazz, who regarded one another as geniuses, realise that their mathematically tortuous music would soon only be a vague background noise for talking and eating to, but such was the case. Edward and his friends were naïvely pleased with themselves for being able to walk into the café and greet other customers boldly, while David shuffled along after them, blinking. Edward ordered corn on the cob for each of them, and also tea which came in tall glasses, with tea bags in them and costing four times as much as in a non-intellectual setting. The waitress was a half caste American Negro who had remained in London when visiting that town as part of a revue. All the young men made a great show of talking to her familiarly, but she plainly regarded them with scorn.

David had been promised the treat of a lifetime, for he was to meet an Urban Guerilla, a fighter for freedom, who had achieved the mighty triumph of being actually *sent to prison* for being found with enough home-made bombs to blow the legs off a whole platoon of policemen.

" This guy's brilliant," whispered Edward. " 'E used to be an architect, but it weren't 'is scene, so now 'e organises like, instead; 'Architect of Destruction' we calls 'im. Anuvver name 'e goes by is 'King Mob' 'cos 'e can organise so well. Shh, 'ere 'e comes."

" Peace and Love," the newcomer greeted them as he sat down and regarded them with burning, hypnotic eyes. David could not understand politics, especially as spoken about in this coffee bar, and he sat aside from the others, as full of emptiness (to coin an Irish-ism) as when he had so tragically lost his mother many years before. Now, to all intents and purposes, he had lost Edward. If only he would talk properly again! David remembered that his father always scorned the idea of one sort of accent being better or worse than another.

" Any accent, rough or high class, sounds pleasant if it's a pleasant bloke or girl talking," Mr Holt would say. " It's people that are good and bad, not accents. Their personality like, gets into their way o' talking."

David agreed with this but now had a rider to add: that slovenly speech leads to slovenly thinking, and hence increases the speaker's stupidity.

Meanwhile, it seemed the ex-architect had just come from a private showing of a blue "art film".

" All these guys screwed this chick one after another, "

he was saying, " yet each guy and the chick, even at the height of it, showed no emotion but stayed cold and mechanical. The least sign that they were having pleasure would have spoilt it all, you see. It would then become bawdy and cease to be Art. "

David shuddered, for though the thought of love-making intrigued him, he was deeply romantic and put the female sex high upon a pedestal. These loveless antics, as described, seemed to him very degrading and he was glad that Art was not one of his subjects.

By and by, the ex-architect pulled out a sheaf of newspapers, some printed upon coloured paper, and handed them around. They were seized eagerly by all within grabbing range, and purple faces plunged into their depths. These papers were of the type known as "underground", and they were intended for the young bedsitter intellectuals who had sprung up at the time when intellect, divorced from all reality, became the sole criterion of success. David took one and scanned it briefly. It seemed throughly baffling to him, written as it was by the fanatical and insane. Every feature contained the word "revolution", used indis-criminately in a variety of senses. Sometimes it meant a violent social upheaval, sometimes a new fashion in pop music and sometimes a spiritual transformation into a Being with super-powers—whether a God or a Devil was never made quite clear. The language and the pictures made David flush deeply and break into a sweat, yet he had not the willpower to put the paper down. The fact that it was legally printed at all amazed him—proof that even a policeman falters with nervous respect when confronted by an intellectual, especially one who can high-falutingly confuse the very different issues of moral and political censorship. Never before had David seen such a barrage of printed obscenity, the words used without pretext. Somehow the pictures of sexual perversions, when printed, made a far deeper impression on his young mind that their counterparts in mens' toilets, which he had always good humouredly ignored. Even a year later, a recollection of one of those pictures would suddenly burst upon him, making him sweat and ruining his mood of happy innocence. He only spent seven minutes or so browsing through the paper, yet for many weeks he could not read the most ordinary text book without imaginary rude words leaping up to assault him from the page. Little wonder that the purple faces around him seemed ghostly, despairing and damned, for their owners read nothing but such literature from morning to night. It was almost as if such reading matter bored a hole into the brain, creating a cave in which the Devil could live and plan his operations.

Almost stunned, David laid the paper down and sat back in his seat. His face became drawn and haggard and as, bar electricity, it would have been as white as a sheet, it now reflected the purple as well as any of the others. Perhaps for this reason, the ex-architect condescended to take some notice of the boy.

" You want to buy this paper? " he enquired, for he was really supposed to be selling them. " No? Do you read a great deal—books, I mean, like Marx and Lenin? "

" Well, what was the last book I read that I enjoyed? " David answered with a question. Now he remembered—

apart from *Winnie the Pooh* it had been *The Vicar of Wakefield*, which they "did" at school, a quaint, charming novel by Oliver Goldsmith. He said as much, adding modestly that he didn't suppose Goldsmith was in the same class as Marx.

"You're wrong!" corrected the ex-architect triumphantly, for his nature was to argue. Having never heard of Goldsmith, he began to lie glibly. "Goldsmith was a drug addict you know, a great guy who paved the way for Marx. There's a most amusing anecdote—Goldsmith was coming out of a café, with Spinoza, when . . ."

He began to ramble on, quickly getting onto politics, until David felt towards him much as did our former Sovereign, Queen Victoria, when she complained that Gladstone always addressed her as if she were a public meeting. Faster and faster came the Niagara of words, each idea, by the loosest thought processes, leading to another idea on quite a different topic which must be expressed immediately before it was forgotten. The speaker's voice became shriller and more hysterical, as he vainly tried to keep pace with the disordered fantasies which tumbled into his head at every split-second. If anyone interrupted, he would seize on their words, misunderstand them and then race off on quite another tangent altogether, before they could speak twice.

David would see the absurdity in some statement, but before he could interrupt to point it out, the breathless orator would be seven subjects ahead of him.

"Capitalism must perish utterly, it must be destroyed in full view of the workers so that they can dance around the flames of the reeking carcase, amidst the foul smell of putrefaction and be there to see its vile skeleton exposed, shorn of the grey flesh of hypocrisy . . ."

" Why? " David managed to put in hastily, turning green beneath the purple.

" Why? Why? Because, my friend, it is based on competition and as the playwright George Orwell most aptly puts it ' the trouble with competitions is that someone always loses.' On the one hand we have the mammoth corporations, wallowing in their millions, wielding vast mercenary power, to say nothing of the brainwashing power of advertisements. And on the other hand the worker and the housewife, helpless, their wage a mere pittance and their power as yet nonexistent, unless we can reach them with our message, penetrate the void, break through the bonds of apathy . . ."

Before David could see the error in this explanation it was too late, but he was to be congratulated for seeing it at all. As he remembered it from school, the competition was not between a businessman and the public, with the public as the loser, but between *different businessmen*— with the consuming public usually the gainer. If only this truth were more widely understood, then people who disapproved of competition would find themselves in the unique position of sympathising with a failed businessman!

As the ex-architect gabbled on with his description of capitalism, couched in the language of necrophilia, David excused himself and ran back to the flat. There he wrote to his father to expect him home any day now. Just as he sealed the letter, Edward and his two friends returned, to sit up all night excitedly talking. David was not to see the ex-architect again for many years, when they met by chance and talked for a few moments.

Next day, David made the coffee as usual and, after awakening his friends at noon, went out on his own to post the letter, and then to see the sights of the West End.

Forlornly and without enjoyment, he paced the baking streets, looking at Trafalgar Square, the National Gallery from the outside, and Downing Street. He had wandered in a circle and was somewhere near Leicester Square when he noticed a British Rail Tourist's Advisory Centre and happily rushed inside to find out how the trains ran to his home town.

Behind the counter was Helen Sheehan!

Before meeting David's astonished eyes, Helen had looked somewhat peevish, and little wonder. A few days before the end of term, she had thrown up her job impatiently and waited for Dick Scuddey either to propose or at least to take her home with him. To hurry him along, she kept dropping hints that she was expecting his child, which she wasn't, and these hints grew so blatant that Dick Scuddey decided to lie low until the catastrophe blew over. Without saying goodbye to anyone, he quickly went home, and nobody seemed to know where his home was. Indeed, a rumour sprang up that he had been rusticated, and it was something of an anti-climax, even to his best friends, when he turned up the same as ever the following term. Meanwhile, this defection had put Helen at a loose end and, when applying at an agency for a job as a translator of French or Russian, she had been advised to join British Rail as a clerical worker. After sundry interviews, she had fetched up in London, where she shared a flat with a nurse in Earls Court.

The sight of David, a member of the university élite, made her remember all her old ambitions and the boy reeled gladly in the face of her flashing smile.

" David! " she exclaimed. " How lovely to see you! "

" Oh-er-Helen! " he gulped. " You're working here now then, are you? "

" Oh yes, but it's only until I can find a place as a translator. This job is all right if you don't mind the public, I suppose, but I don't like it. The public—honestly! You can keep them. It would be all right if you could treat them as they treat you, I suppose. "

A member of the long-suffering public then entered and made an enquiry about the trains to Barnstaple. Helen rolled her eyes up in the air in mock anguish as if to say " Well, really! " and gave David a con-spiratorial glance. David felt glad that he, at least, appeared not to be a member of the public. It seemed to suggest that he was something special in Helen's eyes and gave him the nerve to suggest to her that they meet later in the day for a cup of tea. She agreed eagerly and flashed her eyes at him once again, leaving him in a state of ecstasy and consequently something of a nuisance to the people he blundered into as he wandered around.

When they later walked along side by side in search of a quiet cafeteria, she showed a great interest in his future and asked him what he wanted to do when he left the university. David wasn't sure but he replied that, in order to be a credit to his father, he would try for the best degree he could get and then see what jobs were forthcoming. This apparently made a favourable impression on Helen, for a moment or two later, she gave a sideways bump into him. Astonished at her clumsiness, he moved a little way away, but a second later, bump! there she went again. By the fourth collision, David thought he understood and taking all his courage in both hands, he also took Helen by one arm. To his joy, she leant against him heavily, and unused to keeping step, they both straggled awkwardly along the crowded pavement. Inside the cafe, she pressed her legs against him under the table. Totally unversed in etiquette, it did not occur to Helen that she was being a little forward, and she acted by a kind of sly and cloddish instinct. David was a bit surprised, but he did not complain.

Each day, in the lunch hour and evening, they spent all their time together, separating only at night to take their last respective buses. After five days of almost delirious happiness, David had spent nearly all of his savings and reluctantly had to go home after all.

"I love you," he told Helen, feeling a bit of a fool. "When shall I see you again?"

"Darling, I'm going to give my notice in and follow you back to university," she replied. "I can get another job and a room nearby. I'll have to work off two weeks, however, and then I promised to spend a week with my parents, in Glasgow."

"Perhaps I could visit you there," David enthused fondly. "Glasgow's not all that far from where I live. Would your folks let me stay the night?"

" Oh yes, I suppose so, but you wouldn't like them. They're very Catholic—it drives me up the wall. I'll write to you, anyway and let you know. "

" It'd be great, wouldn't it, if I could stay with you! My Dad's fixing me up with a holiday job as a van boy in his firm. I wasted all last vac. in writing essays that weren't even marked, so I'll not make the same mistake again. By the time I come up to see you, I'll be loaded with brass! "

" Oh David, it'd be smashing to see you! My Dad's sure to agree, and you can stay for a week if you like. "

They embraced in parting and David, for years a dutiful bookworm, lonely and reserved, felt suddenly as if he were a man, with red hot blood in his veins instead of ink and water.

" Let's get engaged! " he exclaimed on the spur of the moment, but though Helen's pudding face broke into a triumphant grin, she did not reply in case of committing herself before a better prospect turned up.

Once home again, David told his father very little about his time in Britain's capital. Edward's new acquaintances were too far from his father's ken to be explained properly, and he shrank from talking of Helen. He had been working for three weeks when his invitation came, and as the letter pointed out that he would have to share a bed with Helen's brother, he felt sure his Dad would approve and showed the letter to him in silence, averting his eyes in embarrassment.

Mr Holt read the letter in great good humour, for he had guessed David's taciturnity to be cover-up for a sweetheart somewhere.

"This lass a student then, is she?" he enquired, sitting back in his easy chair with an air of great indulgence.

"No Dad, she's a translator."

"My, my. It's a wonder what education can do nowadays. We never 'ad jobs like that when I was a young 'un. You'd better tell 'em in the depot tomorrow that you'll be winding up your job. Switch the telly on, there's a good lad, and I'll fix us up a cup of tea in a moment."

It was David's first time in Scotland, and he was glad that Helen was there to meet him at the station. They boarded a bus and went upstairs, where David had his first view of that amazing city. He could hardly believe his eyes at the sight of the grey blocks of tenements, their numbers painted in white on the stone walls near each large, arched open doorway. In these doorways in front of the various dark narrow staircases, children and housewives stood in clusters, talking very loudly— in fact, almost shouting. On almost every corner, in huge whitewashed letters, were painted up the baffling codes and territorial claims of the street gangs who had long been a tradition in the town. The passers-by, mostly shabbily dressed men with hard, unshaven faces, looked to David as if they had stepped from some old Charlie Chaplin film. One tramp particularly caught David's eye, a bearded man with a long dangling scarf and a bobble cap on his head, who carried a staff before him in the eighteenth-century manner. From the nails hammered into the top of the staff hung his various possessions—ragged bags full of rags, a polished kettle with other odds and ends inside it, a tiny oil stove and a spare pair of boots. He was the only person in the whole bustling scene who did not look rather excited. Above all this un-English activity, thick wads of trolley bus wires and other cables stretched across the sky much as in photographs of American cities that David had seen. It was an ugly vista, but one so full of robust life as to be exciting.

Helen bit her lips in anger at seeing David's interest, for she did not at all appreciate having a birthplace that other people considered to be "quaint".

" It's all new where we live, " she explained archly.

David soon saw what she meant, for the Sheehan family had been rehoused ten years before, on one of the many new estates that swamp the countryside on Glasgow's borders. Raw pale brown council houses and blocks stood off from the wide main road, surrounded by open hedgeless grass lawns. The main road was wide and empty, as the English planners had supposed that as the people prospered, so they would buy motor cars. However, the people of Glasgow, though they work hard, do not prosper greatly, for a city run by planners and council house authorities is not very conducive to free enterprise. Those who *do* prosper, however, having no real home of their own, take their prosperity to the pub with them and return without it. Anyway, the huge road was dominated by the one bus among myriad cyclists, like a trout among minnows.

They alighted and Helen led the way among the rows of houses, each with a small and bare front garden.

David still looked about him as if he were a foreign tourist, much to Helen's annoyance. For one thing, this council estate was different from the many he knew in his own distict. The inhabitants were not all subdued or resigned, as on English estates, but strode about vigorously, greeting each other in the broad accent that David found so hard to understand. Children played ring games on the grass verges, scrambled up walls, and sang and danced and skipped to strange tunes that he had never heard before, such as "Keyhole Kate from Gallowgate". Although David did not know it, the estate had been built to replace a most notorious Clydeside gangland area whose picturesqueness was now much mourned by the Glaswegians. In a very short time, the new estate had become just as notorious and gang-infested a district, and with a stigma attached to its name that seemed impossible to remove. Almost every dwelling in Glasgow was council-owned, including the tenements, and the people had forgotten any other way of life. On becoming engaged, couples put their names down for a flat immediately, as a matter of course, and married as soon as the flat was ready. Strangely, in the face of all this bureaucratic manipulation, the bold Celts responded by asserting their own personalities to the utmost, mostly in matters concerning religious differences and football, on which topics the gangs based their very seriously felt philosophy. Reformers had always looked on Glasgow as a "problem city" and one day someone must disclose why Reform leads so swiftly to violent bands of young men roaming the streets. Probably it is because Reformers can only concentrate on one topic at a time and hence make everything lopsided. In Glasgow therefore, the people were housed, but entertainments were few and shops, outside the city centre, were non-existent among both tenements and new estates.

" Why's everyone all crowding up to that van? " asked David in bewilderment.

" It's the mobile shop, of course, " Helen muttered curtly. She was sure her family would make such a bad impression on David that he would never speak to her again. He was her first non-Scottish boyfriend that she had taken home, and she had not quite realised how strange everything would be to him.

" There's oor Helen! " shouted a voice, and a sturdy young boy of ten ran up to them, clad in a grey pullover and grey short trousers. " Is this the young man youse bringin' home, Helen? "

" Go along in, Victor and don't shout in the street, " Helen snapped, while David smiled at the boy.

" It is him, right enough! I'll tell Dad to make ready! " the boy shouted, and scampered off towards a nearby two storey house, which looked very like every other house in the standardised street.

" You'll have to excuse my family, " Helen said quietly from between gritted teeth.

" This way! This way! " called out young Victor, hopping about in excitement at having a stranger courting their Helen and staying in the house a whole week.

" Good evening sir, " Mr Sheehan greeted David, for whom he already had the greatest respect, for in that council area, "scholars" were rarely met with, and Englishmen almost never. He rose from his seat with a kindly smile on his crinkled face and extended the most enormous hand David had ever seen. For years Mr Sheehan had wielded a pick in a coal mining village, before settling down in Glasgow as a short distance lorry driver.

" It's a pleasure to welcome ye into oor home, sir, " Mr Sheehan pursued in an accent partly Scottish and partly Irish. The Sheehans had connections in both Scotland and the fishing villages of Northern Ireland, and this particular branch felt itself to be as much Irish as Scottish. Mrs Sheehan was as plump as her husband was wiry, and it was easy to see who Helen took after. David mumbled politenesses to them both and Mrs Sheehan arose and waddled to the kitchen. She looked like a typical farmer's wife with her round face like a moon with dimples, her curly short hair and her round pink bare arms. The rest of her ample figure and legs were partly concealed by a very large blue and white apron. In fact, she had been a farm girl when first she aroused Mr Sheehan's attention.

" I've a fine bit o' supper just waiting on you in the oven, so you just sit yourself down at table, " she told David, who soon found himself tucking into great heaps of chips, omelette and bacon, with Mrs Sheehan filling his cup with tea as fast as he could drink it, and buttering bread for him.

From his armchair, Mr Sheehan looked on approvingly, his eyes twinkling. David wondered how Helen could have described him as a rough, brutal man. Mr Sheehan definitely saw himself as head of the household, and as in all families there were occasional scenes and some underlying tension, but all in all it was a happy home. In vain, Helen rolled her eyes about in mock anguish as was her wont, and tried hard to include David in her scornful amusement for her parents' simplicity, but the boy took no notice. Here he felt, was domestic bliss, and he wondered if he and Helen could ever live so cosily together. He did not notice Helen's furious silence and, as her parents had to entertain him themselves, he was kept busy in deciphering their difficult accent. Mrs Sheehan asked him the price of bread in England and was disappointed when he did not know. Her husband asked him what team he supported and when David returned the compliment, he gave a surprised smile.

" Celtic, o' course, " he said. " Didna Helen tell you we wuz Catholics? Look there in mah wee flower pot! "

David looked and saw, on the windowsill, a carefully tended bright green shamrock growing from soft earth. Supposing it was a clover, he gave a baffled smile, but actually Mr Sheehan had brought it over specially from Ireland. It was not for a day or two that he untangled the meaning of his host's speech as quoted above. As anyone from Glasgow or Belfast could have told him, the Celtic team is identified with Catholics, and its great rival, Rangers, with Presbyterian Protestants. In turn, these two religions stand respectively for the two Irish political factions whose extremes are the violent I.R.A. on the one hand and the dour Ulster Orangemen on the other. Although a good Catholic, Irish rebel and Celtic fan, Mr Sheehan took his convictions with a solid pinch of humour, almost as a kind of game.

This saving grace of humour, more apparent in the lively Catholics than in the quieter Protestants, might perhaps be because of a vague realisation that these quarrels, which cause perpetual scandal, are merely an interesting and exciting way of passing the time. For most of those involved in them, after all, do not go beyond talk, and in Glasgow the street fighters who take them further are regarded by both factions as being quite "beyond the pale".

When he had eaten, David was invited to sit on the settee, and space was made for him among the various newspapers and comics that lay about. The television was on, but nobody watched it, and the family sat reading papers and chatting in a very relaxed manner. It was an over-furnished front room, for like most housewives, Mrs Sheehan could not resist buying brightly coloured cheap ornaments and pictures, in her case mostly acquired from Catholic gift shops. Nevertheless, the room had personality, for some was bound to rub off on it from its occupants. Young Victor had perhaps a bit too much personality, and his father twice had to reprimand him in a severe awe-inspiring tone— once for taking without asking and once for asking without saying " please ". In spite of these transgressions the boy, when indoors, was unusually polite. Soon a friend called for him, and they rampaged off into the streets together. David found that the contrast between indoor and outdoor manners was quite usual with the children of the district, who combined respect with cheekiness in a most original fashion.

" Helen tells me that you are studying, sir, " Mr Sheehan said to David most politely. David felt somewhat embarrassed, both at being called " sir " and at wondering how his host saw his relationship with Helen. Helen had told her father little about his guest, but Mr Sheehan hoped David would bring some educated new blood into his family. He supposed the youngster to be a Protestant, but his oldest daughter had married one as well, and such defections only added to the spice of life.

" Yes, I'm studying Economics, " David replied timidly.

" Ah, a kind of politics, is it not? The country runs on Economics like an engine runs on steam, I understand, and when the engine runs too fast it breaks doon—now aren't I right?—and only a clever politician can under- stand the workings and how to put it right. It's above the knowledge of me and mah old lady here. Perhaps then sir, you can help me with the workings of mah crossword puzzle? "

David had a flair for crosswords, and he and Mr Sheehan finished the puzzle in no time, to the latter's admiration. Mr Sheehan's opinion of Economics, one conveniently put about by politicians for their own benefit, was the standard viewpoint held by almost everybody up and down the whole British Isles.

" Aye, youse'll be mebbe Prime Minister one day, " the patriarch continued, lighting his pipe. (Helen and her mother were washing up and whispering together in the kitchen—that is, Helen was whispering and the guileless Mrs Sheehan was amiably shouting back to her.) " It'll be a nice change, a decent lad like yourself for P.M. That'll shake up the blue-bloods in London right enough. These blue-bloods and show business folks, ye know how it is, they have sae much money they go spoilt and take to crime and drugs for their variety, so to speak. Such men have been the ruin of old Ireland and that's the truth. Now, if youse gets to be a high-up, you try and set old Ireland free while ye're aboot it."

David had an uncanny sensation of falling into a chapter of his old school history book, and in his confusion said nothing.

"I know well what you're thinking!" Mr Sheehan exclaimed triumphantly. "You think if all Ireland was one, under the true Church—the Catholics, I mean—then the Protestants'd be given a hard time. But it is not so, for we would surely leave them all in peace. Don't look so serious lad, for I say what's on my mind, but never grudge any man his opinion. I have one mixed marriage in mah family already."

As if on cue, Helen returned and behind her came her mother. She sat down close to David, and Mrs Sheehan offered the boy some newspapers to read. To Helen's discomfort, her possible future husband became so absorbed in these as to take no notice of her at all, but sat engrossed, occasionally rocking and chuckling to himself. This was because Glasgow's local papers are chock full of interesting tit bits of news and information, presented in a cheerful homely style, but more so because of their truly excellent comic strips. David once more could enjoy the creations of artists who had illustrated the old comic books of his childhood—who, following the decline of comics in their greatest form, now remained North of the Border. As well, he found the advice columns to be fascinating:

"Dear Problem-Solver. Since my husband passed on,

my eldest no good son has been skulking around my farm although he knows well that I told him he wouldn't lay hands on so much as a penny . . . "

No sooner had David finished the papers, than Mr Sheehan brought out the family photographs and, when David had admired these quite sincerely, then Mrs Sheehan showed him her scrapbook of coloured post-cards she had received. It was maddening for Helen, because she had an awful suspicion that David was not making fun of her parents, but was actually as simple as they were.

Just now he was listening keenly to her father's description of the tracks he had seen on the Irish coast which St Patrick's boat was supposed to have made when it ran aground. Then he turned to Mrs Sheehan and spoke well of the coloured postcard she showed him depicting the mummified head of the Blessed Oliver Plunkett. Unaware of the raging emotions in his loved one's breast, David was thinking that he had never met such nice people. Perhaps when he married Helen, they would live in such bliss together, as he could become a Catholic and live in Glasgow. To David, Glasgow was the most exotic town he had ever visited, and he felt towards its inhabitants much as Lawrence of Arabia felt towards the Arabs. He would learn their ways and become one of them, so as to be a real credit to Helen.

This might not be as hard as one might suppose, for Irish Catholicism is closer to chapel Nonconformity in many ways, than to the gorgeous Madonna-wielding and bejewelled Popery of the Mediterranean lands. For one thing, the Pope seems only dimly aware of

Ireland's existence and for another, the Irish Catholics are opposed to aristocracy and all it stands for, for the "blue-bloods" of that tragic island have been long associated with oppression and religious persecution. Hence, in denying the value of aristocracy, the Irish Catholics all too frequently show a ribald scorn for high society, classical art and everything associated with manorial splendour. So because of the singular failure of aristocracy to "catch on" in Ireland, we now have a Catholicism allied to a rather censorious outlook towards the "high ups" that could easily remind David of his home-town Methodism. Say "We are all simple folks" in a rather smug tone, and you may catch something of the mental atmosphere.

Goaded by dirty looks from their beloved daughter, in the meantime, Mr and Mrs Sheehan began to shift about with a view to going out for the evening. Young Victor returned, but as it was already quite late, he was sent to bed with a pile of comics for company.

"I'm off to the Irish Club, so I am," announced Mr Sheehan cheerfully, avoiding his wife's eyes. His poor wife seemed for a moment almost on the verge of tears, for she had hoped that she could go out with him, but the Irish Club was a very masculine abode.

"It's an awfy long time since we went oot together," she lamented, but her husband made his getaway. She herself threw a shawl over her head, tied it up and declared that she would take a bus into town and catch the last Bingo game, for this was her greatest hobby.

Just as Helen was giving a rapturous sigh and trying out a seductive glance on David, her brother Willy returned, delaying the departure of her mother. David was pleasantly surprised to find out that Glasgow contained a still greater store of Sheehans. In the family album, he had seen pictures of a soldier son in Borneo (a country of whose whereabouts the elder Sheehans were unaware) and of a couple more elder sisters whom he supposed were married off already.

" I won mahself fifteen shillin's at cards, " Willy announced with a certain proud defiance. He was a small, yet good looking teenage stripling, with freckles and restless dark eyes.

" Yer father'd kill ye if he but knew ye wuz gambling! " exclaimed his mother excitedly.

" Och! " said Willy scornfully.

" Ye might well say ' och! ' Now here's your sister Helen's young man come a-visiting, so you mind yourself while I goes out to Bingo. "

With his mother finally out of the way, Willy sat down and smiled openly at David, offering him a cigarette. Helen watched helplessly as the two young men took a great liking to each other. David was still somewhat reeling from the pleasant shock of finding that Scotsmen still said "Och". Up till now he suffered from the school-imposed illusion that everyone everywhere was exactly the same and only pretended to be different to attract tourists. Why, if Scotsmen could say "Och", then Mexicans could wear sombreros, Eskimos could wear fur hoods and savages could wear bones through their noses! A whole new picturesque world seemed to be waiting for his exploration, for, in a way, his visit to Glasgow was his first trip abroad. How different were the natural manners of these

Glaswegians to the forced peculiarities of the young educated cranks of Notting Hill!

"You leaving school soon, Willy?" asked David.

"Och, I'm fifteen, man. I'm a welder's apprentice at Clydeside. I've a mind though, to leave when I'm older and become a fisherman out in Ireland with me grandfather. I love drifting, ye know. When I've no work to do, I like to drift all along by the Clyde, walkin' for miles, ootside the toon all along away."

David looked admiringly at the young hero, envying him his early freedom and independence. Apparently the custom of staying on at school for years and years to please the teachers did not apply in this strange new land. What a country!

"Go and tidy your room, Willy," ordered Helen sharply. "You'll be sharing with David here tonight."

"Och!" grinned Willy good humouredly, and no sooner had he gone upstairs than the bell rang. Rolling her eyes in a frenzy of self martyrdom, Helen answered it to find her married sister had popped in for a chat, complete with her young husband on her arm. Now she gave up, and reverting to her Glasgow manner, she introduced Fiona and Andy and sulkingly retired to the kitchen to make tea. She felt very let down, for she had counted on David to be her ally against her " impossible " family.

Fiona was a tall, forceful girl of some beauty, who wore glasses and very dark red lipstick. She sat close to her husband and kept giving him the teasing and mock-bullying glances and exclamations that showed how proud she really was of him.

Andy himself seemed the picture of strong, honest

worth, and with rather a swaggering sense of humour added, for although a hardworking factory hand, he was now the black Orange sheep of the family. With a beaming smile he pushed his way straight to David and shook hands with ceremony.

" So here's the brave lad who's walking oot with oor Helen! " he exclaimed with the roguishness of a best man on a bachelor night. " So you found a sucker then, Helen? "

David looked confused at such untoward jollity and sensing this, Andy changed his manner entirely to one of grave sincerity.

" Seriously, sir, " he continued, " I'm hoping that you enjoy your stay in our fair city, and that you don't take too bad an impression of us Scots home with you to England. We say what's on our mind up here and sometimes we even add to it, but all of us are in this United Kingdom together to sink or swim. "

" No religion here, nor politics! " pleaded Fiona.

Nevertheless, Andy began to talk about soldiers, his favourite subject. David had never thought about the Army at all before, thanks to the leftward bias of State education, and he sat agog as Andy told of his charging at Arab crowds in Aden, armed only with a transparent shield and a truncheon which he whirled about his head. To his wife's amusement, he rolled up his trouser leg to show his one war wound—a mark caused by an Arab brick. From there he went on to describe the Siege of Derry, which David gathered was before his time. A very entertaining speaker, fond of his subject and of his own voice, he discoursed on armies ancient and modern, from the troops of Alexander to the proposed disbanding of the Argyll and Sutherland Highlanders, which last he took as a deliberate affront to Scotland. By the time the tea arrived on a tray adorned by a colour photograph of Castle Drummond, he was extolling the merits of bagpipe music. Waving a sugar spoon, he next broke into the Orangeman's anthem— "The Sash My Father Wore". Fiona retaliated with one verse of "Kevin Barry" sung in a high clear voice, and Willy ran downstairs bawling out "The Song of the Clyde". David was both astonished and delighted.

"We've no told you we wuz moving, Helen," Fiona continued chattily, as if the sudden burst of glee singing had never been.

"Aye, and it wuz mah doing, too," said Andy ruefully.

"Och, Andy, and it wuz not your fault!" cried Fiona in her lilting accent. "You see, Helen's man—David I mean—we wuz stuck in oor new flat just by the way and the van not coming for four days, so we wuz oot of groceries. Andy works oot of toon in the new factory, so's he could hardly get any, an' me, I didna dare go to the bus stop as that end was where the gang fighting wuz going on. So Andy took the morning off to gae with me, and the road wuz full of young men. They wudna let Andy pass, so he skelped one hard on the jaw just as the poliss came. That was God's mercy, for they wud o' used razors for sure. Andy wuz rounded up with three ithers, and the magistrate bound him over, for he wudna see no lawyers at all. Now the Council heard o' this, an' so they's moving us to some older block o' flats—the tenements, ye know. We wuz there before, but we got good points for behaviour so they let us get a new flat. Och—I dinna worry, we'll get good points again an' be sent off somewhere else."

"Next time, Fiona, we'll do what your father has done," Andy said, putting his arm around her shoulders. "We'll get in their good books and get so many points we'll be allowed to buy oor house off of them, at so much a week on the rent."

"Dad's been paying for years, and it's still ages before he gets this house," Helen commented rather drily. "Ah, here he comes now! Oh no—it's Frances."

Yet another Sheehan had come home to roost, this time the middle sister who still lived at home. It was as well that the house came with three bedrooms. David guessed correctly that the Catholic ban on birth control partly accounted for the extraordinary amount of Sheehans. It also accounted for the harmony among them, for unlike a non-Catholic family, neither partner could blame the other for any new arrival from Heaven. God, in His infinite wisdom, had decreed that families would be large, and who were they to question His holy word? Children grew up relatively untroubled by exams, as they were expected to leave school early and help to contribute to the family purse. Helen had broken with this tradition and she was looked at rather askance, though with some measure of respect thrown in. Frances had done the correct thing and now worked in a chip shop from whence she returned late every evening to sleep till noon next day.

As she seated herself on a pouffe near the fire, crossing her shapely, elegant legs as she did so, David felt he had never seen anyone so beautiful before in all his life. Her hair hung down over her shoulders in ringlets of copper-brown, and her arms were bare. She puffed at a cigarette and looked at him musingly and mischievously. High cheek bones, bold eyebrows and a scattering of freckles set the stage as a backdrop for the greatest attraction—her eyes. These were green and, surmounted by a gentle curve of lashes, they seemed to send out waves of sensuality pulsing towards David. He felt he was being mesmerised and that Frances was a mermaid, for indeed her eyes were like a summer sea and recalled the old fairy stories of seal maidens rising from the ocean.

Frances, besides being a flirt, was rather wanton in her airy and detached manner. No one ever quite knew what she was thinking, but the year before she had presented Mr Sheehan with a totally unexpected grand-child. Her father was very shocked and took it badly, saying that she had disgraced them all. He would not speak to her, but instead consulted the priest who arranged for an adoption. Told of this almost as she went into hospital, Frances' fatal eyes grew wide first with anger and then with tears, but when the parting came, she threw no tantrums. Since coming home, she had been more inscrutable than ever. Mr Sheehan's conscience troubled him then and he grew surly, but the priest assured him that the little boy, Robert, was happy in a good Catholic home. In time the family scar had healed, Mr Sheehan again became genial, and Frances went back to work as if nothing had happened. From then on, curiously enough, she had never been warm, and sat with the fire on two bars even in the height of summer.

David began to sweat, but still gazed at Frances, who in a quiet dead-pan voice was describing the good time she had enjoyed at Hogmanay, the Scottish New Year. For five days she had lived riotously on Scotch and shortbread, sleeping where she fell in crowded flats all over Glasgow. Each day a new party was announced and she had found herself there without quite knowing how. Finally she had staggered straight into work from another party, as pale as a ghost and not knowing what she was doing.

Vying with Hogmanay stories became general and when Mr and Mrs Sheehan came home, they joined in the boasting with zeal.

That night, David thought yearningly of Frances, as Willy, in the same bed, talked softly of the exciting world of the strike-bound Clyde.

Next morning when David arose at nine, he found the house empty except for Helen and for Frances who was still asleep, as she worked from four in the afternoon until midnight. Victor, who had a small bed to himself in Willy's room, had gone to school, and the others were all at work. Mrs Sheehan had a job as a cleaner.

Helen sat in an easy chair, her hair in curlers and an expression of murderous brooding intensity on her face. Her little eyes seemed to be quite taken over by their dark, venomous pupils. David recoiled in shock, but this was actually her normal early morning look and was cured by coffee. In a witch-like croak she asked David to go into the kitchen and make some.

"What shall we do today?" David asked her with forced brightness.

"I don't care."

" Oh. What time does Frances get up? "

" Oh, I've just remembered. My mother asked me
to go into town and do the messages. The errands, that
is, I mean, " she corrected herself, fearful of "going
native".

At the bus stop there was a large queue of housewives
gathered from all over the shopless wastes. Once they
finally reached the town centre, however, then Helen
cheered up completely. She bought the groceries in
a trice and then spent the whole day window shopping
around the big stores, much to David's boredom. They
even had lunch in a big store, but when the shops were
finally shut, David insisted they see some of the more
unique sights, so they went to the Cathedral. David
prowled around its solemn splendour, thoroughly
enjoying himself, but Helen announced that it " gave
her the creeps. " She stood impatiently near the doorway
gazing hard at a postcard depicting the actual view
that lay ahead of her.

While she gazed, her little mind was ticking over fast.
She had half decided to ditch David until Frances had
turned up to provide an element of competition. Why,
she wouldn't put it past Frances to follow David back
to England in term time! After all, Frances had been away
from home before, when she spent six months as a bus
conductress in Oxford, returning pregnant. Frances, she
was sure, didn't really want David, but only wanted
to make sure that she, Helen, did not get him. The two
sisters had been catty towards one another for years
and, futhermore, Frances was never happy until every
man she met had fallen in love with her. At that point,
Helen made up her mind to marry David and force him

into being a big moneyed success, just to show Frances where she got off. So when David was finally surfeited with blue stained glass and brown carved wood, she took his arm and leant against him with all the fervour of their courtship in London. David was very pleased and smiled all over his face. From then on, Helen was very sweet to him, no matter *how* well he got on with her family.

That evening, Mr Sheehan brought out all his record collection and the front room rang with the sound of fiddles. All the Sheehans took Celtic music very seriously, and danced about as if wringing the maximum of enjoyment from every note. There were American hillbilly records and those of Scottish balladeers and dance bands, but Mr Sheehan's favourites were the Irish tunes. Each song seemingly had a story, and Mr Sheehan happily told the story to David as the song began.

One song, a few hundred years old, was against the English but Mr Sheehan kindly told David not to take it seriously. Another, composed a year ago and sung in similar vein, mourned the death of footballer Jimmy Thompson. David thought he had never before heard music so haunting, poignant and yet buoyantly gay, as if of someone smiling through tears. Irish and hillbilly music had merged, and the sweet notes of country violins blended well with guitars, pianos and even harps. David patted his knee in rhythm as the others did, and the songs sent a prickly feeling up his spine and into his scalp. One minute he wanted to cry and the next to laugh, for the songs moved him in a way the folk songs at university could never do.

Strangely, the source of this invigorating music was

the same as that of folk music, for both derived from the traditional songs of unsophisticated people. The folk singers wrongly assumed that the traditional source had run dry and that only they, as Left wing intellectuals, were now equipped to revive and then carry on the heritage. Should a folk singer condescendingly drop into Mr Sheehan's Irish Club and sing a verse of "The Sash My Father Wore", he would be most disagreeably surprised at the vitality of traditional music. Traditional music would not be dead, but he would be.

All over the world, in the meanwhile, including even Ireland, astute businessmen realised that money was to be made by enticing popular local singers and traditional musicians into turning professional. Thus an ex-peasant would record peasant songs to sell to other peasants and more especially to those who had emigrated to faraway cities and felt nostalgic. So the various traditions of music would receive a tremendous impetus as singers competed, introduced new effects and instruments, and learned techniques from recordings of singers made in different countries altogether. These exciting developments were ignored by the arty folk-singers, should they ever happen to learn of them. Everywhere, traditional music began to change rapidly from age to age, these changes reflecting the times in general. Yet the core of the music remained the same. Even as one singer's records became so sophisticated as to be indistinguishable from ordinary popular music, another raw country boy would be leaving the farm for the recording studio. The music that now thrilled young David was a modern continuation of the songs once sung to the ancient Irish kings.

Suddenly the gaiety of the occasion was interrupted by the crash outside of a dustbin being overturned. Everyone ran to the window and peeped through the crack in the curtains. A gang fight was taking place outside, and the Sheehans seemed most interested. David felt the warmth of belonging to a clan and the togetherness of being besieged inside the tiny council-house.

" Ah look, would you—they're trampling down all poor Mrs Macpherson's fence, " cried Mrs Sheehan in indignation, but to her disappointment the fight straggled off into another street. Only Mr Sheehan seemed irritated and unmoved by its occurrence.

" Nobody has a good word for these gangs, " he complained, " so it beats me where the gangs come from. Folks roon' here complain o' gangs the way other folks complain o' bad weather. What is the use, I ask you, what is the use o' yon Council buildin' pubs if ordinary folks here can't go inside them for fear o' the gangs? Do you not have gangs in England, sir? "

" Not where I live, " David replied. " We just have trouble outside the pubs on Friday an' Saturday nights. There's boys in leather jackets, but they only seem to sort of stand about. "

" Oh aye? Happen this area's just got a bad name and that's an end to it. I can't blame oor Helen for wanting to quit. "

Helen smiled and took David's hand coquettishly.

In the days that followed, Helen repeatedly told David that she loved him. At meals she stroked his legs under the table with her foot, and, whenever Frances was present, she closed David's eyes by kissing him passionately and shamelessly. Frances kept a cynical silence even when, on the day before David's departure, Helen announced to the company that she and David would be getting married as soon as possible, while he was still at university. David grinned very foolishly and looked at the floor, while Mr and Mrs Sheehan fussed over him delightedly. From then on Mr Sheehan addressed him as " David ", although he still sounded rather humble.

David wrote to his father and told him the news, adding that he would bring Helen back with him for one night, which he himself would spend on the sofa. Mr Sheehan saw him and Helen off at the station and even carried their bags for them, despite their half-hearted protests.

" Once I've taken you people to the station, I'll drop into Mass before I go back, " he announced, as they waited for the bus.

David looked at his shabby clothes in surprise and asked if his church was near the station.

" Mah church? " he echoed with amusement. " The whole Catholic Church is mah church, ye ken. It's not like you Protestants—no disrespect intended—who each have a special church like a club, that they dress up for in a suit and all. No, we Catholics, we go to any church nearby, and in oor working clothes or any sort o' clothes at all, and we are all welcome. The Man in the Sky don't care *what* sort o' clothes you wear, after all. Still, I suppose with your way it's only custom. "

With a wise chuckle, Mr Sheehan began to sing over and over again a rhythmic line from an Irish song: " It was not for the want of employment at home. "

Helen, who often said while at the university that she

" believed in Man ", offered up a prayer, presumably to Man, that the bus would soon arrive. David looked at the dismally planned estate all around him and idly scanned the peculiar inscriptions on the front walls of houses, inscriptions which the householders had long given up trying to remove.

" That's gang rubbish! " Mr Sheehan said with biting contempt, following his gaze.

From the top of the bus, Mr Sheehan gave an entertaining commentary on the streets and landmarks that they passed.

" I know these streets so well, as I drive mah articulated lorry all roond here every day, " he commented. David wondered at how he could drive so bulky a vehicle around the narrow turnings, but Mr Sheehan, with modest pride, explained that it was only a knack.

As the happy couple boarded the train, Mr Sheehan bade them both farewell with great courtesy, shaking David's hand firmly.

" Goodbye Dad, " David told him, and his eyes lit up in his weather-beaten face. Helen, for her part, placed a hand over her eyes as if on the point of fainting with exasperation.

Mr Holt had bought a whole lot of cakes, fruit pies and ice cream to welcome his son's fiancée. He was very taken aback at the news and he grinned at the couple in acute embarrassment. His old-fashioned home and his Northern lack of pretension were a great disappointment to Helen, and her own smile was very false. She behaved as if she was slumming and trying hard not to burst out with some comment on the ridiculous way in which the poor lived. For David's sake his father tried to like her, but he couldn't help noticing that whatever he said, she fluttered her podgy hands in the air in amused amazement and rolled her eyes up at Heaven and then round towards David to include him in the joke. David himself was far too happy to notice anything at all. What joy to be married into such a fascinating family as the Sheehans!

That night, David did indeed sleep on the sofa, but Helen behaved as she would never have dared to have done in her own house, and tiptoed down to join him. Mr Holt guessed what had happened and was not very pleased, but he said nothing. As for David, he was now in such a rapture of love as to be a lost soul. Later next day Helen departed for the university town to look for a room and a job.

It seemed so strange and unreal for David to be back at university after the momentous occasions in the holidays. Helen was there to meet him, having found an office job and a room nearby. Together, they went to see the Vice Chancellor and explained that they were getting married that term. Abstractedly, he told them that there were no married quarters as yet, and they would have to find a flat in town. He also gave David an application form for an extra grant to support his wife, and then there was a pause as David and Helen waited to be congratulated. Finally they left.

In the Social Centre, the furniture had been piled up outside in the hall, for a Trade Union dance was in full swing, complete with a brassy orchestra. Students were not invited, but Dick Scuddey was there as his parents were honoured guests. Scuddey senior proved to be a fat, bull-necked red faced man of great coarseness and an air of immense self satisfaction. He clutched a bottle of wine in one hand, waving it above his head and roaring with laughter. His hard faced wife was rather more prim, and Dick Scuddey already seemed to be scorning them both.

When Helen had gone, David sought out Edward, who now looked the complete anarchist, as did most of his friends. They talked wildly of the promises and predictions of the ex-architect, and David could see that Dick Scuddey's spell was broken. In a dim way he began to realise that the moderate ideas of Dick Scuddey, when carried to their logical conclusion, led to the insanity of the ex-architect. At the moment, these ideas were carrying all before them, but though David had no better ideas, he was too preoccupied with Helen to be swept along with this latest tide of fashion.

Within a week, he and Helen had found a flat and paid a deposit down upon it. It consisted of two rooms and a kitchen, situated over an ironmonger's shop in a new and unlovely shopping street, made of brown tiles and white concrete. Helen thought this was really smart and they bought some furniture on hire purchase and made ready for their life of bliss.

At last, almost a year from when David had left school as an ardent train spotter, the great day dawned. Rather wistfully, David had asked Helen whether she thought he ought to become a Catholic, but Helen pooh-poohed the suggestion and they were wed in the registry office in town. Mr Sheehan, who paid for the reception, was also disappointed at this but he hid it well. There was quite a crowd in the drab little building, as the Sheehans, the Holts and another bridal pair and

entourage all sat in the waiting room. A festive atmosphere was lacking, as everyone was reminded of a
doctor's surgery. Mr Holt was there with his scandalised
chapel-going sister-in-law and his eldest son who was
to act as witness. The latter had brought a very flashy
tall girlfriend to keep him company. The Sheehan
contingent were represented by Mr and Mrs of that
name, two of Helen's aunts, one with husband attached,
young Victor and Willy who stared around in amazement, and Fiona and Andy. All had taken time off to
make the journey, and they would take the night train
back. Frances had yawned and declared that she couldn't
be bothered to come, but that she wished Helen all the
luck that she would need. Non-related guests consisted
of Edward and two friends, whom David had beseeched
to have their hair cut. After much soul searching, they
had trimmed it off within reason. Helen apparently
had no friends.

David was very nervous and he sweated and paced
up and down. Helen, on the other hand, looked smug
and content as she chatted to one of her aunts. Mr Sheehan
and Mr Holt had taken a liking to one another and sat
and chatted quite easily, commenting favourably on
one another's offspring.

A clerk appeared and called Helen, David and the
witness out for a dress rehearsal. Helen's dress, by the way
was white but otherwise secular, and she had bought a
bunch of flowers to pose with for the photographer
afterwards. David wore a navy blue suit and he looked
as smart as always, but flustered.

The Holts, Sheehans and others, including the other
bride, groom and company, all sat in the tiny dark

little room and waited until David returned as white as a proverbial sheet, to say that they were now ready. David glanced yearningly at his Dad, almost as if wishing that the latter could remain his closest living relative. He wondered if he was doing the right thing. Helen, on the other hand, was very self possessed and she was fortunate in having met David when he was almost fresh from school, and regarded women as remote mysterious goddesses.

The guests all stood awkwardly around the office room, seeming ill at ease but determined to be cheerful. Helen, David and his brother, all very well dressed, stood apart from the others before the registrar's large oaken desk, covered with official forms and documents, that did duty as an altar. The registrar was a mild-mannered fat man, with glasses and wispy hair. Making little jokes to break the ice, he led tactfully into the matter at hand. When he announced that the room had been " blessed and sanctified by a bishop in Holy Orders ", Helen gave a little jump and looked annoyed, while David looked terrified.

Soon, the deed was done and the whole crowd surged outside for the photographs. David and Helen were one and that one was Helen, who looked almost fiercely triumphant. David looked sheepish, as most bridegrooms do, and the other young men seemed to think the whole affair was a joke, as most bachelors do. A stern notice in the hall banned the use of confetti inside or out, but no one took any notice and soon the couple were ducking and grinning as the stuff was showered over them. Outside, the hired photographer awaited them with an air of smooth politeness and their rash act was recorded for posterity, against a background of flower beds, sapling trees tied to poles, and municipal benches.

Fleets of taxis then transported the crowd to a Chinese restaurant in the centre of town, for the reception. Helen and David usually dined here and had a sentimental liking for the place. They had explained to the delighted manager that English chicken dinners, with soup and sweet fore and aft, would be the most acceptable, with champagne for all. Fortunately, Mr Sheehan had saved to give each of his daughters a send-off and, sadly for him, none had yet chosen a Catholic. Now only Frances, a very dubious commodity, remained unwed and in a position to strengthen the clan by fresh Catholic blood.

Each of the guests had a printed card in front of him or her, and the row of tables were liberally adorned with flowers. Chinese waiters, all smiles, gaily flitted about, clearly enjoying the gala occasion. The reception was held in an upper room, but even so, the Oriental setting came as rather a surprise for the middle-aged guests, who had never been in such an establishment before. None of the Sheehans, except for the bride, had ever so much as thought of eating Chinese food, which they vaguely supposed to be dogs and cats. Happily, the food was sufficiently Westernised to reassure them.

Both the Dads made short, bluff speeches when the toasts came, each in turn referring to " my daughter " and " my son " with obvious pride. David, when his turn came, could only blurt out " Thank you, thank you! " and sit down. Mr Sheehan went pale as he examined the bill, but he paid manfully, in notes he had earlier drawn from his Post Office account. Mr

Holt, who had promised to help the couple get a house when David's course was over, looked thoughtful as he wondered what to cut down on. It was a disappointment to him that his son could not afford a honeymoon, but faced with a choice, Helen had decided on a well-furnished flat in the modern style.

A flurry of kissing, congratulating and calling of taxis marked the end of the reception. David felt somewhat dazed, and regretful that during the confusion he had not managed to say very much to his father. Still, now he had a wife instead and he supposed he had better make the best of it. Soon they were home in their flat and he looked at his better half rather nervously. She put her head on one side and looked at him in an amused, quizzical fashion, her long hair dangling. His new life was about to begin.

Several terms later, David could be seen hurrying to and from the university with files and papers under his arm, for he was now working very hard. He could barely remember the time when he read comics and drew pictures of Winnie the Pooh, for he was now a fully fledged Man of Responsibility. His finals were not far off and he had a wife to think of, although a very lazy one. Helen had never yet learned to cook or sew and she never worked for more than a month or two at a time, preferring to lie in bed and read magazines. Nevertheless, David was devoted to her in a rather dogged, singleminded manner, and neglected almost all of his old acquaintances. Sad to say, these last included his father, whom Helen discouraged him from seeing.

However, he spent a great deal of time with *her* family in the holidays, always enjoying himself greatly. He had persuaded himself that he was an honorary Glaswegian, even picking up a touch of the accent and fairly glowing with tribal loyalty.

During the term, David, as a married student, took very little notice of his co-scholars. His once alert and perceptive appearance grew dulled, for he had long ceased to question the notes he learned by heart, or to set any value on the truth when it ran at variance to his lecturers' creeds. After all, he was there to pass exams, not to understand things. In a way, his studying had made him stupid, but in another way it had made him cunning, for he had to anticipate his lecturers' views.

Unthinkingly, he strode into lectures, stepping over the rebellious protesters who lay about on the floor. These, in defying the lecturers, had become twice as ridiculous as David, who tried to please them. They plastered the walls with notices of complaint and revolution, but never ever thought of leaving. One of these notices ended with this statement: " Next thing, the Administration will even try and stop us having *sex*, if this authoritarian trend continues. "

As the above implies, girls had become more frequent in the last two years, and now they strutted fiercely about the place, their little baboon rumps sticking comically out from beneath their minutely short skirts. Their rooms were mixed in with those of boys quite indiscriminately, with no attempt at discipline. Dick Scuddey was still around, and had caused a sit-in strike in favour of the new Union Building being completed earlier than scheduled. Nevertheless, he had been quite eclipsed by the fantastic ideas culled from the ex-architect, which were too imaginative for him to understand properly. Edward had become a wild-eyed convert and had spread the gospel enthusiastically and with great success, for it filled the empty, lonely vacuum in the souls of most of these State-graded scholars. Henceforth, all the fashions were political, and the worse the trouble-maker, the greater his prestige among his fellows.

Edward's squinting eyes now burnt with a fanatical light and he quivered and spluttered with zeal. He had even tried to grow a beard, but it would not progress beyond a fringe of fluff. Every day and most of the night, he held political meetings in the corridor outside the television lounge. Despite the comfortable chairs only a few yards away, all the radicals sat on the floor, disrupting traffic and causing confusion.

" Revolution! " they shouted, if anyone wanted to get past. This seldom happened, for as everyone liked community chanting, most students were inclined to join in their " meaningful dialogues "—to quote the college magazine. For the participants, it was most stimulating, but for the cleaners it was quite exasperating, as the " champions of the poor " habitually left the place littered with so many heaps of old torn newspapers and leaflets that it resembled a beauty spot on Bank Holiday. Furthermore, some of them kept communally owned dogs, which presented a pitiful appearance as well as adding to the general mess.

One glorious day, Edward discovered that the canteen orange juice originated from South Africa, that land of apartheid, or perpetual torture. After a fiery harangue on the demerits of the fascist orange juice, he led a mob that surged into the Administrative Building and occupied it. They daubed the walls with painted slogans and kept up a monotonous chant of " We're gonna sit! We're gonna sit! We're gonna sit, sit, sit, sit, sit! "

When asked by the Vice Chancellor to leave, they demanded the instant dismissal of the caterer, an elderly family man. This was ignored, but happily for Edward and his followers, the Press heard of it and reporters arrived to interview them. From then on, Edward and the others considered themselves to be immensely significant, and for the first time they felt proud of their university, as it now took its rightful place along with the fashionable colleges of America as a place of strife and violence. At last, student life had some meaning and they knew why they were there—to pose before the television cameras. The caterer was forgotten as fashion followed upon fashion. These fashions aped the rebellion of American youth against institutions which did not exist in Britain, and so had no purpose but that of wild enjoyment. Edward envied the American rebels for having draft cards to burn and police to shoot at them and he copied their language as well as he was able.

Lectures were seldom disrupted, as the new militancy was used to occupy their free time—" Satan finds work for idle hands to do. " However, the more Communist of the lecturers now came into their own, and many were the meaningful dialogues.

Surprisingly, when the finals were over, both Dick Scuddey and Edward obtained Firsts, while most of their followers got Thirds; David ended up with a

Lower Second. Edward's success could be attributed to his phenomenal memory, while that of Dick Scuddey was thanks to his encyclopaedic knowledge of the Trades Union movement. As for David, who had muddled through by half-learning the accepted formulae in undigested chunks, with great effort, he was now faced with a new emergency—the outside world. Nearly all the students now faced this grim reality and not all of them were lucky enough to postpone it by means of a post-graduate course. It was most unfair, they felt. Just as they were beginning to really enjoy university life, they were expected to leave! Few of them had ever thought about jobs, as their ambition had been simply to go to university, and the rest of their lives would be an anti-climax.

Edward had learned, to his intense rage, that his bad eyesight and long hair prevented him becoming a train driver. Happily, he had the idea of sending away for contact lenses, which he paid for by borrowing off his uncle. (His father was out and about, but though Edward now boasted about him, he still held him in fear.) When the contact lenses arrived, they were duly inserted under his eyelids and had the effect of making the eyelids swell baggily and the whites of his eyes turn red. After much inner turmoil, he sacrificed his principles and had a shave and a haircut. Then he presented himself at the station master's office nearest to his uncle's home. There he was told that to be an engine driver he would have to first start out as a porter and slowly work his way up. Eagerly, he agreed, but when the station master heard of Edward's qualifications, he was horrified and threw up his hands at such folly!

Expecting that Edward might have one G.C.E. to his name, he found the would-be porter was a Bachelor of Science! In no time, he had entered Edward for the clerical examination and, upon his passing brilliantly, he coaxed the reluctant boy into taking a post as a filing clerk, with his name down for a managerial course.

David, eagerly spurred on by Helen, was more ambitious and asked all his lecturers for advice. " Industry, " they said, and gave him boring pamphlets. However, his history lecturer was very keen for David to work for the Trades Union movement and arranged an interview for him as a Liaison Officer. Feeling very nervous, David mumbled and stumbled his way through this and lost his chance by forgetting the date of the Taff Vale decision. As he tottered from the room, he passed Dick Scuddey who, with a triumphant stride, brushed him out of the way brandishing a letter of introduction from his father.

Some of the students actually *did* go into industry, to the detriment of the latter. Others became school-teachers, deck chair attendants, insurance clerks, bus conductors and labourers. Some of the girls, who considered nudity to be idealistic, became artists' models and one became a prostitute. This was an Irish girl who had become somewhat deranged due to losing her faith, a seeming inevitability in a university. The lucky students were those who were enabled to stay on and eventually become lecturers themselves. Almost all of the students suffered from the same disability— a bad interview manner. Their grammar schools had not taught them to present ideas rationally in debate or discussion until the sixth form, when it was too late.

By then, they were either too shy to speak one word in public, or else they would get carried away by an undisciplined imagination and gabble feverishly. To these initial handicaps, the university had added others. For instance, the idolisation of the working man and the American Negro had added so many quirks to their speech as to make it virtually unintelligible to a layman. Compared to ex-public-school boys, these unhappy scholars were like gruff, shambling yahoos.

Edward had spoilt his accent, so that he failed every managerial test one by one. The procedure was to invite all the candidates for a social weekend at a country house and to assess them for manners and deportment as much as for stored up information. As Edward believed manners to be hypocrisy and clear speech to be snobbery, he had forgotten how to pick up on these vital assets to civilisation, and startled everyone by his involuntarily uncouth and boorish behaviour. Back to the filing office!

David was not unduly dismayed at failing his interview, as he shared his father's dislike for Trade Unions, though Helen was very peeved at this setback. The newspapers were so full of vacancies, however, that they did not despair. Mr Holt had raised the money for a mortgage down payment and the couple had promised to repay him bit by bit. So their whole future was mortgaged and *Helen* now wondered whether she had done the right thing. Frances had gone off to live with someone, far from trying to steal David from her. Oh well, she supposed she'd have to try and make the best of it—at least she'd achieved her ambition of escaping from Glasgow.

" I've just had a thought, Helen, " said David, shortly after he ceased to be a student. " Let's decide where we're going to live first, and then I can get a job nearby. What part of Glasgow can we get a private house? "

" *Glasgow* ! " shrieked Helen, nearly collapsing. " I'm not going to live anywhere near *Glasgow* ! "

" But what about your family? We want to be near your family, after all. "

" You speak for yourself. I've had all I can stand of my family. It's me you married, not them—we'll see far too much of them as it is, at Christmas and so on. Honestly, I sometimes think you only married *me* because of *them* ! "

This was so true that David was silenced and Helen began to talk hastily of a house with a garden in Surrey or Middlesex, and a job in London. She talked long and shrilly; and when she had at last finished, he felt quite bowed down. Glumly, he made tedious and expensive pilgrimages from their Midland flat to London's West End, following up vacancies for graduates. Jobs, so profusely advertised, seemed to be sparingly handed out, and all London teemed with graduates. At first he had wondered whether universities shouldn't have careers officers, instead of leaving the bewildered students to sink or swim. Later he realised that employers were ignoring students from the newer and more obscure universities and, in all honesty, he could not blame them. Until asked some pertinent question by an impatient manager or personnel officer, he had not realised how boundless was his ignorance.

Meanwhile, the situation was becoming desperate. Helen supported them both on her office girl's wages and as she was very careful about money, they both lived off baked beans. Every time he had to borrow the fare to London, to be told by some employer that they'd let him know, his wife looked so martyred that he could not bear it. It was at this time that she acquired the habit, so galling to David in later years, of going off the deep end whenever they were out together and he fancied a cup of tea or a sausage roll. At his wits' end, he applied locally for teaching jobs, but they all seemed to be filled, somewhat to his relief.

On his fourth visit to London, he arranged to meet Edward, who soon convinced him that he too could become a filing clerk, with greater prospects ahead. Before the week was out, British Rail had acquired an additional member to their staff. David, who was now house-hunting in the suburbs, was told that he could start as soon as it was convenient, and his life's work would begin at Waterloo Station.

Edward, in the meantime, had been ignominiously dismissed from the railways for his prolonged leaves of absence, as he still careered around Notting Hill Gate until all hours with his old cronies from the blues clubs. Again he took a room and grew his hair long, announcing that he was going to be a writer. Life on the dole, he found, was very much like life as a student once more, and it was what really suited him, although he found the grants weren't quite so good. A beautiful but dopey girl soon came to live with him, and they sat about in the nude, talking rubbish about Art and Politics and feeling very pleased with themselves.

For David and Helen, the clouds had passed and the sun was shining once more. They were householders at last!

Their chosen lovenest was a small and rather flimsily built mock Tudor house in suburban Surrey, a delightful neighbourhood in the summer, with the birds singing and the gardens blooming. It was the beautiful garden that had attracted them to the property, but unfortunately, in their innocence, they thought that it would look after itself. As the weeds rose and the flowers wilted, the elderly man next door grew very perturbed, for he loved gardens. It was two months before David and Helen noticed him and then he at once offered to do their garden for them.

"You young folks are always busy," he said earnestly, "but I'm retired, so I could come in and do it while you were away."

Surprised, they both agreed. Helen declared that their neighbour was "a conformist who wants our garden to look like all the others," but David felt ashamed and began to mess about in the garden himself. Helen still went to work, but at home she was incredibly lazy, and all their meals came from the chip shop. Each Sunday they spent in bed, with scattered newspapers falling here and there. Helen was firmly on the pill, although David would have liked children, and this chemical addiction seemingly made her nervous and irritable. Nevertheless, they were not an unhappy couple, as each had mentally vowed to make the marriage a success. Gradually, they grew alike in their ways and were reasonably contented, although they had few friends. David enjoyed his job and joined the station football club.

If ever he felt he was missing anything by living in suburban domesticity (which *was* rather a come-down after the high hopes of university) he would go and visit Edward in Notting Hill. Edward now regarded him most patronisingly, and finally David ceased to keep in touch, satisfied that the fashionable world of rebellion was not for him.

On what was to be his final visit, Edward was lying on the unmade bed with his very pregnant girlfriend curled adoringly up next to him, as if marvelling at what a mighty brain her man possessed. The brainy one looked very severe, as if about to shoot a speculator, and delivered lectures at David, allowing no interruptions.

" The problem that faces the world is the population explosion, " he ranted. " In Britain alone there are fifty thousand homeless families, who are a top priority Government problem. "

David reflected that the only homeless people he had seen were old tramps, and the authorities made it harder for these by removing seats from railway stations and closing down library reading rooms.

" You do not see these homeless families, " Edward continued, as if sensing David's thoughts, " because they may have homes, yet these homes are such that normal family life cannot continue in them, therefore the families are homeless. The reason there are all these homeless families is because of the worldwide population explosion in India and China. My plan, which will need a world government, is to lay down by law how much each person may eat, and to allow only one child to be born in each family. People may kick at first, but it's the only way. In my book, I have set out in detail a rigid Thousand Year Plan. After a thousand years of austerity, the restrictions will be ended, and the world can once more be fully enjoyed. 'Ere, Doreen, pass me that dog-end, will you?''

It was now a peculiarity of Edward that his official speeches were in crisp, vaguely American tones, while his normal speech was still as slurred and disagreeable as ever. Gladly, David escaped, first wishing the frowning Edward luck in his literary career.

How sweet did Surrey seem after this metropolitan excursion!

Mr Holt was now alone in his little house in the faraway North, but at least he felt he had done the best for his family. David's house was cheaper than he had expected, but when he saw it, after they had moved in, he understood why. It had been built in the early part of the 'twenties, in a slip-shod manner that was now illegal. He foretold to himself that they would have trouble with damp and he noticed that the awning around the door was only made of plaster. In size, it was not very different from his own house in Providence Row, but its appearance was odd, as the small Greek pillars in front blended strangely with the black painted brickwork that simulated Tudor beams. Still, as with his own house, which he had bought when the old landlord had sold out, it had the saving grace of being inexpensive. Nowadays, private builders could not sell to the poor so easily, and in his district, almost all the new houses were council owned.

These practical matters apart, Mr Holt felt somewhat sad and puzzled in the way David had turned out.

Without a word, he had rushed into marrying this superior translator girl and now he scarcely saw him. It had all been so quick, and now David scarcely seemed the same person as the bright little boy who had watched him at work, banging and sawing, with such interest and pleasure. Nor did David seem to understand Economics, for he never spoke of it any more. When people asked Mr Holt what David was doing now, since leaving university, he felt rather silly when he told them the boy was a clerk. Still, in his childhood, a clerk had been a most respected person, and he supposed that the wheel had gone full cycle. The modern education has certainly changed everything, for now even the big shops in town expected their young assistants to have some exam results. Vaguely, he supposed that the modern education must be wonderful, if you couldn't even do the most ordinary, easy jobs without it.

David and Helen, or Mr and Mrs Holt, soon forgot their earlier ambitions and lived for the day when their house would be entirely paid for. In time, Mrs Holt rather mellowed and even felt herself looking forward to Christmas and Easter, when they went to stay in Glasgow—as long as they didn't stay *too* long. On their first anniversary, they managed a short and belated honeymoon in Cornwall, but they worried about their house and were glad to be back. They hired a colour television and on it they watched Dick Scuddey, now a Labour M.P., making a fool of himself. As he hurried to and from the office, David sometimes felt he was missing something, for his older suburban neighbours, before they retired, had often led the most exciting lives in various outposts of the Empire, as it then was.

But when he read in the papers of the violent riots in his old university, he was glad that he too had left his days of excitement behind him!

The Painter and the Church

for

CAPTAIN LEARMONTH

Many thousands of years ago, in what is now Central France, lived a small community of about eighty individuals known as the Bison Tribe. These worthy and hardworking people, hunters to a man, lived, at the time of which I'm writing, in and around a series of caves in a rocky, scrubby countryside—an intermediate zone between the dark, deep forest and the open plains. Those who could not be accommodated in the caves, lived as best as they could in furze huts nearby. A fallen tree, with spreading branches, afforded an ideal adventure playground for the many children, where they could disport themselves in comparative safety, within sight of their mothers who sat gossiping and working in the doorways of their homes. Their housework consisted chiefly in the cutting up and skinning of game, and sewing skins into warm, furry tunics and boots, with the aid of bone needles and threads made of sinew. Now and again, an infant would fall off a branch, or receive a deadly insult from an erstwhile comrade, and run crying to Mum, who would usually comfort it by popping a lump of delicious bison fat into its open mouth. Such consolation made grievances almost a pleasure, and well-satisfied, the child would toddle back to its playmates. The older children, aged ten to fifteen, helped their mothers, if girls, and if boys, hunted wild beasts, such as black grouse and hares, with real bows and arrows.

The men divided their time between hunting and, with great self-importance, discussing religion. All women's work was naturally beneath their dignity, though if any woman shared this view, it was their solemn duty to chastise her. Religion and politics were inextricably entwined, for each tribe had a different shaman with powers over a different animal. The Bison Tribe were firm allies of the nearby Reindeer Tribe, had a current peace treaty with the far off Wild Ox Tribe, an uneasy peace with the mysterious Bear Tribe, and lived in outright fear of the ferocious Wolf Tribe, who lived in the deep woods and followed a cult similar to the Leopard Men of modern Africa. Compared with the poor Reindeer Tribe, who were always coming and going, following the herds, the Bison Tribe led a contented, settled life. The bison, who were somewhat dim, would frequent a relatively small area for two or three decades before noticing they were being killed left, right and centre—whereupon, they would seek pastures new and the tribe would follow them. Of course, members of the tribe were allowed, even encouraged, to kill other animals than bison, but bison were their speciality. They believed in a patron saint of bison, and they alone knew the correct rituals in hunting and preparation of meat and skins that propitiated this Being. The Reindeer Tribe knew the correct rituals for reindeer, and so on, as well as the best ways of transforming skin and bone into exchangeable goods. Now and again, meetings were held which were similar to both markets and religious conferences. Bison, ox, reindeer and occasionally bear products were traded, and the whims and peculiarities of each patron saint were discussed, with a view to mutual co-operation. Every animal had a soul, they believed, and who are we to call them wrong? Upon being killed, the creature's soul supposedly flew straight to its patron saint, who received it hospitably. If all rituals had been carried out correctly, the soul would give a good account of its slayers, and offer to serve them again. So, after some days of feasting, the patron saint would clothe it anew with fur, flesh and bone, and wishing it good luck, send it back to the forest. All the patron saints came under the jurisdiction of God, the Creator, and Giver of Meat. He it was who had created the forest, plains, mountains and sea, and then peopled them with beasts, birds and fishes. This He felt was not enough, and so He made three attempts at producing humans. First came the small, stooped Beast-Men, who were hairy and inarticulate, and hunted with sharp bone daggers. This was clearly not good enough, so a second try produced the Small People, who were men of a kind, and inventors of the bow and arrow, with which they drove the Beast Men far into the wilderness, so that now you seldom saw them. However, perfection was only achieved with the creation of them, the Bison Tribe, Reindeer Tribe and so on, who being large and aggressive, chased the Small People into forbidden and haunted sectors of the forest, and took over the hunting lands. The Tribes had one divine gift in common, which raised them in status from four legged animals almost to demi-gods, and that was the possession of Art.

If anyone showed huge talent in this field, which then consisted of music and painting, he was expected to serve the community as Shaman and peacetime Chief, and was apprenticed and trained accordingly. Skill in fashioning hunting weapons from bone or flint was a practical, rather than a divine gift. A Shaman or Shaman Trainee was not expected to be a hunter, but to be concerned with spiritual matters alone. Of course, in those materialistic times, spiritual matters were all connected with the getting of meat, but in fact the Church provided a respected niche for those of artistic temperament. Every tenth autumn, at a tribal congress, a new Shaman was chosen, and the old one relegated to assistant and advisor.

The present Shaman of the Bison Tribe was an old man of fifty, named Kimmak. For the last year, he had worked alone, but recently he had apprenticed a young boy named Aktuk, whom he hoped would take his place in two years' time, when his term of office expired. Aktuk had a natural talent for painting, and his help was already invaluable to Kimmak, who was grossly overworked. This being peace time, there was no military leader, and a good thing too, thought Kimmak, who was a pacifist by nature. Military chiefs tended to be the toughest and most unreasonable of all the tough, unreasonable young men, and to have a habit of badgering the Shaman for ridiculous charms against the enemy. As if a Shaman hadn't already enough to do! For instance, there was the manhood initiation in a moon's time, and pictures to paint and ceremonies to perform. The medical side of things he left to the tribe's Wise Woman, a formidable old lady with an extensive knowledge of herbal remedies, fertility drugs and midwifery. She had a healthy scorn for all manly activities, Art and hunting included, and he avoided her. He himself was a widower, with a crinkled kindly face peering from beneath the hair of his bison horn headdress. As badge of office, he always carried a bison tail, which he flicked briskly about, using it as a fly switch. To ensure the respect of his parishioners, he even took part in the occasional bison hunt—because they *did* respect him, they always made sure he never got hurt. Most of his days, however, followed the same pattern. In the morning, he and Aktuk would go out and hunt for the roots and mud necessary for the making of paint. At noon they would eat, being offered the choicest cuts by housewives grateful for the good hunting they'd provided. Then they would mix the paints, using bison fat as an ingredient and a bison's shoulder-blade as a palate. Kimmak had perfected a deep reddish hue that had made him famous. Aktuk had a gift for spotting a rock formation on the cave wall that resembled part of a useful animal, and they were soon both at their labour of love, independently creating huge portraits of beasts whose souls were worth possessing. For it was part of the Faith of all the Tribes that a lifelike portrait gave the painter power over the subject's soul—power which he could transmit to the tribe at large, if he were a Shaman, by means of the ceremony held every seven days. Portrayal of a recognizable member of the tribe was therefore unheard of, and theoretically punishable by death. Use of the sacred instruments—drums and picking bow (which latter had a banjo-like effect)—meant banishment, and all secular music was played on bone flutes alone. Flutes were a recent craze, and had no place in religious ceremony, but in general, Art was not for Art's Sake, but entirely for the Divine Purpose of worshipping God and providing meat.

Happily, Kimmak and young Aktuk worked side by side. They seldom spoke, except to shoo away any inquisitive person who strayed into the sacred hunting temple (a cave with a good wall for painting on) with lofty explanations of the artist's need to be alone. Later, at dusk, they'd have finished and would proudly exhibit their masterpieces to an admiring tribe by the light of burning flares from a perpetual fire the tribe kept going.

"Aahh!" everyone would gasp in admiration and anticipation, and Kimmak would ask everyone to especially note the grotesquely fat stomachs that were his trade mark, and that he hoped would ensure good eating for the whole tribe for many a moon to come. Then off the two artists would go, to any household they chose, and sit round a fire eating roast meat, telling stories and hearing other people's, and perhaps listening to some young man playing the flute, though Kimmak never really approved of this habit.

After supper, it might be the evening for a hunting ceremony, and then Aktuk would go home to his mother (his father had perished during a disagreement with an elk) for he wasn't permitted to attend ceremonies until after his manhood initiation. If he had attended one, he would have been surprised to see gentle old Kimmak, his scrawny body concealed in a complete bison outfit, leaping around like a madman, all the while playing a picking bow, while others thudded out a bloodthirsty rhythm on drums. Of course, he could *hear* all this, and shuddered, and pulled the bison robe bedspread over his head, wondering what spirits were loose. Meanwhile, Kimmak danced and danced, until finally he was possessed by the spirit of the patron saint of bison. The spirit, paying no regard to the tired old body it was inhabiting, began to shriek to the young men of the tribe to seize spears and kill the bison. This they did, until the night air rang with the clash of spears against stone, as each animal portrait seemingly quailed beneath the onslaught of blows. Nervous young men of recent initiation might fumble their aim, overawed by the combination of rhythm, hunting fever and leaping firelight shadows. Then others would scornfully direct them to the "beginner's pictures"—animals with their hearts and vulnerable parts clearly indicated, as if in X-ray. After five or six hours of this, the hunting fever would have overcome any judgment the crowd might have possessed, and at the crucial moment just before they might have started throwing spears in each other, the spirit would leave Kimmak and he'd slump to the ground. As if by an order, the music then stopped and the party broke up. Someone helped the exhausted Kimmak to a pile of skins, and, tired but still excited, the men would go silently to their homes. In the dawn, the spirit's exhortations still ringing in their ears, they would leap up from their beds, snatch a spear and be off to the bush fearlessly to attack a bison or any large beast they might encounter. Unless more than one of them surprised a bison at the same time, there was little teamwork in their hunting. The individual family had sole rights to the skin, but the meat had to be shared with the needy, and also a gift had rightly to be given to Kimmak, who had inspired the whole project and who also would be feeling very frail after the night's exertions.

It was easy to see that Aktuk had an artistic temperament. For one thing, he had an unusual fear of wild life and the wide open spaces. It terrified him to be out of sight of any other member of the tribe, even for a moment. The games the other boys played, all concerning hunting or fighting, had no interest for him at all. His greatest childhood pleasure was scratching pictures on walls or bits of bone, often inventing little stories of hunters and hunted, somewhat in the manner of cartoon strips. As custom dictated, the humans in these dramas were mere stick figures, but the animals made up for this, for he gave them very human features and expressions. This gift earned him some respect, even before Kimmak had ordained him for the Shamanry in hot bison blood. Since his ordination, however, his Mum and tribe mates had ceased to badger him about learning to hunt and other athletical activities. Like many a modern Mum, Aktuk's parent had resigned herself to being the mother of an intellectual—a being that was currently useless, but who might win great glory later on. She was a faded, resigned-looking little woman, with her hair in a bun with a bone running through it. Her two grown-up daughters had married into the Reindeer Tribe, and she felt rather bitter that they never came to see her any more. As Aktuk was incapable of work, being small, weedy and lazy, she was dependent on charity. Once she hoped that Aktuk could be trained to cut up meat — properly a woman's job—but this he did with such blithe disregard for religious convention that an angry visit from the Wise Woman resulted. Did Aktuk's Mum want sterility, pestilence and famine to fall upon the tribe? Hastily, Aktuk was told to run out and play. The Wise Woman had disapproved of Aktuk ever since he had proved her wrong by surviving at birth. Luckily, Kimmak adopted the boy not long after this, which raised his mother's status immediately—all the neighbours began to congratulate her on her brilliant son.

" We knew he'd go far, " they told her, forgetting that days before they had whispered to each other about how drab and pitiful she looked, but what could you expect with no husband and a half-wit for a son?

Aktuk too was pleased with the change. He had never been before in the sacred hunting temple, and while his solemn ordination was to him just so much red tape, he was delighted to discover the secrets of mixing colours and the joys of splodging them about. In no time, he equalled Kimmak as an artist, though his style was somewhat different. Kimmak's animals stood fat and stolid, ready to be slaughtered—a hunter's dream, in fact; while Aktuk's were lean and running, with an eager, smiling expression similar to that of Aktuk himself. It always annoyed Aktuk to see the scratches and smears inflicted on his darlings by the hunters' spears. Could it be that the principle behind his work was lost to him?

Unknown to anyone but himself, Aktuk was suffering acutely from the pangs of calf-love. The adored object was a perky little girl of his own age, named Alianak. Unlike most tribal maidens, who prior to marriage affected many sophisticated airs and graces—painted faces, bead necklaces and beaver-skin gloves—Alianak wore only a large handed-down hairy skirt, when the weather was fine. This was three sizes too big, and therefore rolled up and tucked in everywhere, and it looked like a bouncing bustle as its wearer jauntily danced to and from the river with a clay jar. Being kindhearted, Alianak always seemed to be running errands for someone, but being also scatterbrained, these very often went wrong. She was a small, plump girl with tangled, straggly hair falling over her dark, bright little squirrel eyes; and her normal expression was one of pleasant good humour. Most people treated her with affectionate condescension, but to Aktuk she was a goddess. For the past year she had been very entranced by his picture-stories that he scratched on bones and antlers for his own amusement. Delightedly, he'd explained to her all the finer points she'd overlooked, and she went " Ooh! " and " Coo! " and "Innit good, eh? " Her eyes sparkled with admiration, and, beside himself with joy, Aktuk presented her with one of the adorned bones. Henceforth she was always popping in and out of his cave, admiring pictures and prattling gossip and often bearing delicious blueberries, that he was too nervous to go into the forest and look for himself. Aktuk never spoke his love, but given time he might have done so, had not Fate, in the grim shape of the Wise Woman, snatched her from him for the womanhood initiation.

After this lengthy ceremony (for though the men never mentioned it, the Wise Woman was really a priestess in her own right) nothing more was seen of Alianak for some months. After this time, Aktuk's rise in the social scale gained him access to many hitherto indifferent families, and he discovered Alianak was very much married. Kimmak had come to reprimand her husband for neglecting certain ritual thanks for the good hunting the tribe was now enjoying. Aktuk came too, and was amazed to find Alianak, looking very harrassed, crouched in a corner scraping a reindeer bone with a piece of flint. He greeted her enthusiastically, but she only gave him a brief nod. He soon understood why, for her husband, who had been shuffling his feet and looking surly in front of Kimmak, wheeled angrily round with a half roar on hearing his wife spoken to with such familiarity. Seeing it was only Aktuk, whom he still regarded as a half-wit, his rage subsided into mere silent contempt. Aktuk's heart actually seemed to pain him when he saw the look of adoring appeasement Alianak flashed up at her husband. Almost in tears, he stumbled after Kimmak—then stopped dead as he heard a loud slap followed by a shriek coming from the cave, as the man of the house reprimanded his help-mate for not preparing the food soon enough. For a wild moment he pictured himself striding back inside and rescuing Alianak from this monster. After all, he reasoned, she couldn't possibly love the fellow—he was too rough and brutal. Then he hurried after Kimmak, who was striding rapidly away, matrimonial problems being no part of his job at all.

A week after that, Aktuk was sitting in the sacred hunting temple contemplating the finished portrait of a wild ox in front of him. It had taken him a long time to complete, as his mind contained nothing but thoughts of Alianak. Dreamily, he noticed that a rocky protuberance upon the cave wall looked just like the top of her head. Picking up a lump of charcoal, he improved the likeness. Then it was, as tribal history relates, that Keeli, the evil spirit of misfortune and bad hunting, took possession of the boy. Almost unaware of what he was doing, yet working feverishly, he first sketched and then painted a perfect life-size likeness of Alianak, showing her in something of a pensive mood. He gazed at his work for a long time, and then some uncomfortable thoughts crept into his mind. The taboo against a human likeness had never been broken before in his lifetime. When it had been broken, as his elders had told him, it had been in time of war, when some unscrupulous young men had drawn pictures of their enemies in the Bear Tribe. This unsportsmanlike approach to war had aroused the wrath of the other, more chivalrous warriors, who protected the pictures from harm by spears, and, tying up the offending artists, pitched them into the enemy camp where they were speedily put to death. A theological problem was created by the existence of the pictures, which was solved by filling the cave in with boulders, and abandoning it. Aktuk realised that Alianak's fate was in his hands. He could kill her if he wished, but naturally that idea did not appeal to him. A grandiose inspiration came to him. If he caressed the picture, Alianak herself would run to his side for similar treatment. Tribesmen would find them together, and kill them both, and together they would enter the happy hunting grounds. He hoped they could use a good artist in the happy hunting grounds.

So it was that Kimmak and three of the fiercest young hunters, entering the cave for a religious purpose, saw Aktuk nuzzling his head against an unmistakable portrait of Alianak. All were stunned, but the most upset of all was Alianak's husband, the largest of the group. Assuming some kind of black magic was being practised on his wife, he sprang at Aktuk with a choking sound midway between a sob and a snarl. He threw the boy to the ground, and would have strangled him had not Kimmak ordered the other two, who were looking almost ludicrously bewildered, to prevent any further desecration of the temple. They pulled the outraged husband back by the arms, but he soon broke free, and turning, ran out of the cave to see if his wife was safe from harm. Alianak, the cause of all the trouble, was found blissfully throwing shreds of meat to a very tame raven that hung around the settlement. This in itself seemed an omen to her husband, but seeing her alive, he again wheeled around and ran back to the temple, sobbing aloud. There he found almost all the men of the tribe—women were forbidden to enter—holding a meeting which Kimmak had speedily organised. Aktuk sat silently, a young man holding him at either side. Kimmak began his speech.

"People of the Tribe, I am as shocked as you are at this sudden and unexpected evil in our midst. However, I must beg all of you to exercise restraint and take no personal action against the boy. It may be, that during his ordination, I made a mistake and allowed an evil spirit to enter the lad. In any case, by tribal law, he is not deemed responsible for his actions until *after* the manhood initiation ceremony has taken place."

He paused and looked around, wondering what to do. An uproar of conversation made it hard for him to think. Outside the cave, Aktuk's mother was moaning her boy's name in a loud despairing tone, vaguely aware that something had happened to him.

"The boy will stay with his mother," this prompted Kimmak to say, "until a meeting can be arranged with several neighbouring shamans to decide his fate."

"Never mind the boy," a young man spoke up. "He has always been mad, as we have often told you. What about the picture?"

"With a wet skin, it can be removed," Kimmak mumbled uncertainly.

"Will not Alianak herself then disappear?" the young man wanted to know. Alianak's husband gave a start at this, but said nothing.

"Let a wet skin be brought," Kimmak commanded. Eventually it was. "Now I want everyone here to pray for our beloved Alianak, as I will myself, and I want you, young man, to remove the picture."

Aktuk looked wildly at the crowd, all of whom were reciting prayer after prayer and staring at the picture. Fearful of the role destiny had cast him for, the young man slowly advanced towards the picture, holding the dripping skin rag at arms length. No sooner had he gingerly touched the picture-Alianak's hair, than Aktuk let out an ear-rending scream, and ran straight out of the cave, nearly knocking over his own mother. Everyone looked at Kimmak, but he merely motioned the young man to continue, and soon Alianak's picture was no more.

Filled with dread, the tribe members slowly walked out of the cave to see what had happened to the real Alianak. They found her unconcernedly sewing some skins together for a tent, and her husband was so moved by this deliverance that he flung himself into bed and spent three days being ill and waited on by his patient little wife, Alianak. Theological discussion raged on into the night, but no one thought to look for Aktuk. He'd never been known to leave home ever before, and Kimmak thought he'd be with his mother, and his mother thought he'd be with Kimmak. But in fact, Aktuk was running far into the forest. His mind was filled with thoughts of Alianak disappearing or dying, and himself being tribally executed with spears or,

divinely, by a thunderbolt. Crying and talking hysterically to himself, he ran madly along an old bison trail,
disregarding the growing dusk and the small forest
creatures diving into the undergrowth at his approach.

Fortunately for Aktuk, the bison themselves had been
harried by his tribe into moving fifteen miles further
away in the opposite direction, and the various
carnivorous beasts that preyed on the young and sick had
followed suit. Even so, the woods teemed with small
game, and when Aktuk's first wave of hysteria had worn
off, he was made uncannily aware of a thousand invisible
eyes watching his every movement. Rounding a corner,
he surprised a red deer hind, and through the last strains
of sunlight, he watched it bound away amongst the
bushes, his heart hammering, for the surprise had been
mutual. Very few of the bravest hunters ventured out
after dark, and darkness was well on its way. Aktuk was
now about two and a half miles from home, and he
decided it was time to make the return journey right
away. His two previous expeditions had done nothing to
make him confident of the wide-open spaces. At the
age of ten, he had been abandoned a mile from home by
the boys supposedly looking after him, who had chanced
on a female elk and given chase, despite their small
arrows being as less than mosquito bites to the great
beast. Luckily for the boys, the elk got clean away, and
as they were triumphantly rushing home to boast of
their adventure, the memory of the weakling Aktuk
stopped them in their tracks. One boy climbed a high
tree, and from there could just see Aktuk scrambling
forlornly about on some rocks, his mouth open wide in
unheard screams for help. Hypnotised by his fear of the

forest, Aktuk had made for this nearby open space, and sat for an hour watching two eagles wheeling around the blue sky. Then getting up and calling for help, he had angered a female bison who had strayed from the herd to give birth to a calf. Leaving the calf to sprawl wobble-kneed in the long grass, the mother had made small snorting rushes at Aktuk, who clambered up some convenient boulders and waited nervously for rescue, which soon came. The older boys easily eluded the clumsy fury of the mother, and pulled Aktuk to safety between narrow gaps in the rocks. After that nerve-shattering experience, he stayed at home for four years, playing with smaller children. But half a year ago, Kimmak had insisted that he take a close look at the living creatures whose portraits he was supposed to paint. They both waded along a small stream, with steep banks, that ran through a meadow the bison were using as a grazing ground. At a signal from Kimmak, he had straightened up and peered through the bracken, finding, to his alarm, a small herd only ten feet away. His job was to memorise individual characteristics of the fattest beasts, but all he'd actually noticed was how fierce they looked, especially the huge herd leader, who had a massive humped shoulder and wicked red eyes. Unexpectedly, four young men with spears suddenly advanced on the herd from a thicket, all roaring like commandos on a bayonet charge. The herd leader had bellowed mightily, and then the whole herd of about twenty beasts thudded their way into the birch trees, passing only three feet from Aktuk and Kimmak.

That day, Aktuk had sworn never again to enter the forest. And now here he was, alone among leaves and

growing darkness. Any amount of torture and humiliation would be worth it, if he could again see fires
burning and hear human voices. Looking up, he saw an
owl, like a miniature black cloud, float across a patch of
open sky, and settle on a branch, with a long hooting
cry. Aktuk turned round and was on his way. It was a
pity, really, that the bison had made so many trails, all
criss-crossing each other, for Aktuk took the wrong
turning and marched woodenly off into the deep forest,
neither looking to left nor right, for fear of what he
might see. All around him, the black grouse, awakened
from their beauty sleep, rocketed up into the trees with
a crash of feather and foliage equal to the sound of a
brick wall being demolished. Aktuk walked on, by now
covered in sweat, which he could feel running from his
armpits in cold streaks. He understood the awakened
grouse to be evil spirits, but he knew that if his stride
faltered, he might sit down and die of terror, which
wouldn't be a good idea at all. The moon came up, and
shed silver bars of light between the trees. Shadows
grew blacker, and lay across his path like serpents. As
tree tops stirred in the midnight breeze, their shadows
seemed to snatch at poor Aktuk, who was by now
repeating the names of everyone in the tribe aloud to
himself, in an effort to keep calm. A bat swooped past
his face, and his resultant scream awoke another battalion
of black grouse. On he went, but now the bushes were
crowding over the old trail, and he began to realise that
this was not the way he came. He stopped to think, but
unfortunately a badger chose this moment to cough
irritably, having choked on a snail, and it followed the
cough up with a grunt and a growl, but the cough alone

was enough to send Aktuk hysterically on his way to nowhere. An hour later, by which time Aktuk was repeating the names of ancestors several times removed, the trail ended in thick undergrowth, which sheltered a female wild pig and her five offspring. Anyone who has heard the squeal of a frightened pig on even the sunniest of days in the safest of farmyards will have some idea of the horror Aktuk experienced on hearing the whole family voice their alarm in that terrible spot. Numb with fear, he fell against a tree, and clung to it with all his might, shouting desperately for help. The noise of wild pigs died slowly away, until all he could hear was his own voice. He shut his eyes, his head spinning, old scenes and voices whirling around his brain. He even seemed to smell a fire and hear footsteps.

A voice said clearly, " Is anyone there? "

Aktuk, who had been dozing for the last two minutes, looked up with a start, and saw a bearded man holding a burning torch and staring at him with the utmost curiosity.

" Of what tribe are you? " asked this stranger.

" The Bison Tribe. Er—you? "

" The Bear Tribe. Are you alone? "

" Yes. "

" You've lost your bow and arrows, have you? "

" Er—yes. "

" You silly boy, chasing wild beasts until the darkness traps you. Come with me, and you can go home in the morning, at the proper time to be in the forest. Your mother will worry, but it can't be helped. Perhaps one day you will be a great hunter. "

Twenty minutes later, they came to a clearing, where

the Bear Tribesman had left a small fire burning, and had a comfortable tent rigged up, made of thick bearskins and a sapling framework. Inside, he even had a spare bearskin for Aktuk gratefully to roll up in for the sweetest night's sleep he'd ever had.

In the morning, the hunter awoke Aktuk with some dried meat. Aktuk was very silent, but the hunter, glad of the unexpected company, talked enough for two.

"You're lucky you met me, young feller me lad," he said. "My tribe are many miles away, but I left to trail the bears deep into the woods, and to find the caves and hollows they are using to sleep and rear their cubs in. I've discovered a mating couple, and today I'm going to mark the trees with my axe, so's to find the place again in a couple of months, with my tribesmen. We'll kill the male, and leave the female to bring more bears into the world. It's a wonderful creature, a bear. Bears are like men, more than any other beast. Do you want to know how I kill a bear? I'll tell you—I find where he'll be, and I take my friends, and we all have spears. We surround the bear, and crowd him in until he has to make a stand of some kind. One of the hunters—it might be me—rushes at the bear with his spear, and shouting. Up goes Mr Bear, on his hind legs, his two big paws raised and his neck arched for battle, with the hairs standing on end. He growls like thunder, and as he lurches forward, right over me, I thrust my spear deep into his chest, jump aside and he falls dead. It's easy really, though of course, I've many scars to tell of my mistakes."

"Are—are there bears in these woods?" faltered Aktuk, perhaps not at his brightest that morning.

" I'll take you to see some right away! " promised the hunter, inspired by his own flow of words. " Come on ! "

" Oh, please don't bother. "

" It's no trouble, I was going there anyway. That'll give you something to tell your tribe, back home. "

So it was that Aktuk found himself crouching among the undergrowth on a steep hillside, staring down into a valley where a small dark cave was just visible among the bushes. The eye of experience, which Aktuk did not possess, would have told him this was bear country, for the animals' perambulations had created a pattern of muddy paths winding here and there through the scrub country. Suddenly Aktuk realised the furry brown object in the cave entrance, which the hunter was staring at earnestly, was actually a sleeping bear. At that moment, the hunter pointed, and another bear, a large dark brown one, was seen slowly approaching with a leisurely, rolling gait, and cropping the grass for all the world like a big sheep. At once the sleeping bear, a male, fat and fawn coloured animal, awoke and in a burst of ardour, lumbered towards his beloved, his large behind bouncing comically up and down. For the next hour, Aktuk watched entranced, forgetting all fear, as the bears carried out a tender and chaste flirtation. The hunter seemed full of simple pride, as if the bears were his own invention. Although a voluble man, he felt a love and veneration for the beasts he preyed upon that he could not express in words. For a long time, the two bears circled each other as if in a ceremonial dance, wheeling around on their hind legs, and rubbing their backs together. Having performed this rite, they would drop on all fours again, rub their necks together and then whirl around, stand up and repeat the procedure. Eventually they rolled blissfully to the ground, both on their backs, the male with his hind legs sticking up in the air, like a tubby child playing dead. There they lay, side by side, licking each other happily. When the female reached out with one paw and pulled her lover tenderly towards her, so that they lay snugly together, grunting contentedly, Aktuk could not but recall the happy dreams he had vaguely planned for himself and Alianak. He did not know it, but the bear's courtship is brief, and their ways soon part—the male even eating his own children, should he encounter them later.

Eventually Aktuk and the hunter tore themselves away, and the latter began seeking an easy route back to the Bison Tribe. With the hunter by his side, Aktuk felt unafraid of the woods, and the wonders of nature revealed to him at every step filled him with a spiritual reverence that Kimmak would certainly have approved of. Finally they came to the river, and the hunter instructed Aktuk to keep to the bank and by sundown he would reach his home territory. On no account was he to take a short cut, as the nearby woods were not only haunted, but also the home of the unpredictable Small People, and the Tribes were forbidden to enter them.

"Have you seen any of the Small People?" asked Aktuk.

"No, but we of the Bear Tribe trade with them. They make many beautiful and magical ornaments, from bone and rare stones, and as well always have plenty of meat and honey. But they do not spear fish, or know how to prepare skins or how to make clay pots.

So we leave our goods at a certain place outside camp, and in the morning they are gone, and in their place are honeycombs, necklaces or meat wrapped in leaves. But beware of them—they commune with strange spirits, probably evil ones, and I have heard that given the chance, they steal babies, either to eat or to bewitch. In any case, they never come out into the open by daylight, so you ought to be all right. Our Shaman says that if they see the sun, they die. "

With these strange stories ringing in his ears, Aktuk and his new-found friend parted, and chewing the dried meat offered as a parting gift, the boy made his way homewards, wondering what to say when he got there. The river bank was fairly open country, consisting of tall grass and alder thickets, but to his left, the dark forest brooded. However, Aktuk trotted on, telling himself what a brave outdoor man he had now become. Every time a water bird squawked or fluttered away, he gave a jump, it's true, but immediately afterwards he smiled at the thought of how silly he'd been. He'd been walking for five hours, and was making his way through a widely spaced out copse of trees, when a terrible feeling suddenly hit him and turned his soul to ice. He stopped, unable to explain the sensation of some alien force of evil that menaced him and filled him with fear from knees to stomach to heart to windpipe. Looking up, he saw a very large wolf, right in his path, and eyeing him appraisingly. It was a well-built animal, standing tall on its pale slender legs, and staring coolly and unflinchingly at Aktuk. Its flanks were reddish brown, its jowls nearly white, and a black, bristly line of hair ran from its backbone to the end of its tail. A magnificent specimen, and not just a pretty face, either, for it was well versed in the ways of man, its competitor in the meat market. For instance, it had noticed that Aktuk carried no weapon, and had begun to stink of fear. An amusing situation. For a while it was deadlock; then the wolf, with what seemed to Aktuk a macabre sense of humour, yawned prodigiously, revealing a beautiful set of ivories, and lolloped a little to one side, taking up a new stance, still observing Aktuk keenly, its head now cocked slightly at an angle. Hoping this meant it gave humans the right of way, Aktuk took two steps forward. The wolf raised one foreleg as if to move on, deliberated a moment, then put the leg down again. Aktuk stopped. Time seemed to stand still. Somewhere far away above his head, a songbird chirrupped. Finally Aktuk could stand it no longer, and walked tentatively forwards. His best friends would have advised him to climb a tree, but they were not present. The wolf affected to lose interest, and began sniffing at some object on the forest floor. Emboldened, Aktuk walked on, keeping a sideways eye on his persecutor. To his horror, he found the wolf was keeping pace with him on a road parallel to his, taking short prancing steps and still eyeing him with great interest. Having had more than its fair share of the good hunting the district now enjoyed, the wolf actually had no malevolent intentions. It certainly relished the feeling of power, but it was also motivated by a strong and irresistible curiosity—a feeling that would lead many of its descendants to become dogs.

Ahead, the undergrowth became congested, and Aktuk was afraid the wolf would use the cover to take

him unawares and make a meal of him. He didn't
dare to turn round, so he began to walk slowly backwards
the way he had come. After a while, the wolf trotted
over to where he had once stood, and sniffed at his
tracks. Then it stood in his path, stock still, and gazed
him out of sight. Encouraged by the wolf's diminishing
figure, Aktuk stumbled backwards faster and faster,
until he rounded a corner and the wolf was out of view.
He pondered the situation, and decided he would have
to make a detour through the deep forest, despite the
hunter's advice, and rejoin the river further along,
when he was far ahead of the wolf. Nervously, he made
his way through the salad-green silver birch thickets,
until he found himself in the shadow of the great, dark
and fearsome pine trees. Here, birds were silent, and
Aktuk could hear his heart pounding. This was the
forbidden forest, where squirrels ate pine cones, pine
martens ate squirrels, and lynxes ate pine martens.
Aktuk wondered what would eat him. A woodpecker
flew past, flashing black and white wings and crying in
fear. Poor Aktuk's heart sank, as, as if in answer to his
question, the persistent wolf again appeared, viewing him
as keenly as before. Just as his knees were trembling
in preparation for a faint, he heard a faint rustling, and
the wolf wheeled around and with apparent nonchalance,
sauntered away, its long bushy tail held at half mast.
Looking about him, Aktuk felt that uncanny and unreal
sensation that you feel when a dream exceeds the bounds
of your credibility and you feel obliged to wake up. For
striding self-importantly towards him, were four tiny
men. Each held a small bow and had a quiverfull of
arrows attached to a loin cloth, made of a hare skin, at

his hip. All were between four and five feet high, but proportioned like muscular giants. Their skin was darker than Aktuk's, and very weatherbeaten, and their expressions were all very severe.

Aktuk stood dazed, while they surrounded him and began poking him roughly with their fists, shouting at him and to each other in high, querulously indignant tones.

"I do not understand. Can I go home now?" he murmured. None of the men took the smallest notice, but began arguing amongst themselves. Suddenly the oldest and sternest of them, a venerable greybeard, punched one of his fellows on the cheek, and prodding Aktuk roughly with his bow, motioned the terrified boy to accompany them into the forest depths. The punched individual walked a little to one side, looking peeved.

(What had happened was that one man had advised leaving Aktuk alone, as his race brought bad luck, but the others all agreed to keep him as a slave, and a majority ruling was upheld.)

They walked on in silence for a very long time, until a clearing in the ominous and hitherto monotonous forest was reached. All the men looked pleased at this, and Aktuk's hopes that the sunlight would kill them were soon dashed. The Bear Tribe's shaman had erred on this point.

Miniature women and children ran forward to greet the returning hunters, and they whooped with astonishment on sighting the strange catch. A highly embroidered story of Aktuk's capture was told, and the poor victim was poked, prodded and generally humiliated. The small children hid; some ran away shrieking; but everyone else was eager to examine this strange trophy. Aktuk was frogmarched up to the large building that served as a combination of village hall, community centre and Salvation Army hostel—this was to be his home, as it was for all the single members of this strange tribe. It was a huge dome-shaped construction, made of countless bent and woven saplings, and a few strategically placed tall boulders. Over these, mud had been packed and then turf, still growing, plastered over the entire building, so it was possible to mistake it for a natural mound in the clearing. Most of the tribe lived in small, hastily thrown together stick huts, which stood under the trees, in a circle around the community centre. Aktuk did not know this, but the circle was powerful magic for the Small People. For one thing, it was the shape of the sun, which they believed to be God as seen from the distance. The clearing, which was actually a long-dried-up pond, was also circular, and although the tribe followed the game and built a stick shanty wherever they were as sunset approached, their magical community centre was never entirely deserted. A scattering of women, children and old men always remained to keep the home fires burning, and it was for their benefit that Aktuk had been introduced. A hole at the top of the building emitted a wisp of smoke, and Aktuk stared at this in amazement—it was the first chimney he had ever seen. He was prodded towards a cavelike opening between two boulders—the only entrance, and into which the men were descending one at a time. Even though his knees shook with fear, Aktuk felt an intense curiosity about the strange company he was in. His emotions were similar to those of someone who, for the first time, is sent to prison. Inside, in the smokey half-light, he found a rope ladder. Hesitating, he was roughly pushed with the handle of a spear, and nearly fell, only just grabbing the ladder in time and hastily scrambling down.

Inside, it was another world. A crackling fire lit up the premises, and Aktuk saw that the grass-covered dome was only the roof of a large subterranean dwelling dug out of the earth. Skins of various animals lay around the one room, stretched over flat rocks that leaned against the walls. Despite the miraculous chimney, the odour of wood smoke was overpowering. People's belongings—bone tools, strings of beads, small drums, various weapons—were all over the floor in a state of great disorder. Around the fire, some crinkle-faced women, their eyes bloodshot from the smoke, sat hunched up sewing skins into primitive pants and waistcoats. These were spinsters, and having no specific husband to wait on, did all the odd jobs in the community and kept the fire alight. On seeing Aktuk, who instinctively gave a polite smile on meeting company, they gasped in loud amazement, and made circular signs with their hands to keep away any evil influence. A short parley with the hunters grudgingly convinced them that Aktuk was not an evil spirit, but a different and lesser race of human being, and more important, one who would do all the work for them. They received this information sceptically, and one of them curtly motioned Aktuk to sit down, and then offered him two skins partially sewn together, with the needle and thread still dangling. Looking very worried, Aktuk began to sew very slowly and clumsily. At once all the women began to laugh and shout, and four of them nearly knocked Aktuk down in their great eagerness to point to him the next place to poke the needle through. Men, women and children were meanwhile pouring and tumbling down the ladder, and throughout all the noise and chaos Aktuk sewed solemnly on. Everyone seemed amazed and delighted at his prowess, as if he was a performing animal of some kind. When he proved unable to bite through the tough olden-day thread, an embarrassed hush fell on the audience, and when he eventually succeeded, it was broken by a huge sigh of relief. At last, even the children out in the forest collecting pine cones for the fire somehow heard about Aktuk, and came swinging down the rope ladder in almost dangerous haste, their mothers rising to catch them if they fell. Once more, Aktuk was the centre of attention. The standard of sewing among the Small People had always been very low.

After an hour or so, the novelty of Aktuk seemed to wear off somewhat, and people began to drift out in ones and twos. Some of the stocky little children had fallen asleep here and there, curled up on the ground. Their mothers awoke them, and the kids whined briefly and then automatically fastened themselves on their mothers' backs in piggy back fashion, and fell fast asleep again, to be carried out of the building. Those of the tribe who remained, looked around restlessly. The spinsters had long given up work, and sat gossiping. Poor Aktuk was very tired and hungry, and worked slower and slower. Some meat was roasting in the ashes, but no one thought to offer him any, or to signal him to stop working. In the end, delirious with exhaustion, he lay down his needlework, seized a piece of meat and ate voraciously. No one took any notice, so encouraged by this, he pulled a piece of leathery hide around him and fell asleep on the floor.

He was awakened ten minutes later by the sound of drums, and then flutes joined in, and he was made dimly aware of dancing figures. With a jolt, he awoke—some religious ceremony must be taking place. As a matter of fact, he was wrong, for the Small People played music and danced for pleasure alone whenever the mood took them. Rubbing his eyes and looking around, he saw men and women holding hands and dancing around in circles, while others capered about playing musical instruments. Now and again, a young man and woman slipped discreetly up the rope ladder together. After a while, a fat bearded man hurried down the ladder looking very important, and carrying under one arm a large clay pot. Everyone ran up to him, and with an air of great benevolence, he allowed each one to take a swig. This gentleman was, in a sense, the local publican, and he brewed a very heady form of heather wine, from some recipe that is lost to us. Seeing Aktuk's curiosity, this worthy allowed him a small sip. Just as he decided he didn't like it, Aktuk changed his mind as a warm glow filled his body. To his great disappointment, he was not allowed any more, but the fragrant smell lingered in the room, helping him mentally to re-live that precious moment. In the meantime, the conoisseurs of good wine were becoming more and more excited. Ignoring Aktuk, they leaped laughingly about, shouting playfully and chasing members of the opposite sex.

Eventually, led by the brewer-publican, who still was in firm control of the drinks supply, they joined up in a kind of conga and danced in single file sixteen times around the hall, some beating drums, and then paraded up the ladder into the darkness and stillness of the forest night.

Dark the forest night may have been, but it soon ceased to be still. Had Aktuk followed the others, he would have witnessed the uncanny sight of nearly every able bodied person in the tribe dancing by moonlight in a huge circle. They held hands, kicked up their legs and shouted, and this resemblance to children playing "Ring-a-ring a rosie" was heightened by most of the company, especially those who had drunk most heartily, falling down every now and again. But Aktuk was too sleepy to become very excited over a primeval Saturday night, and once more he curled up for the night, the sounds of drums, flutes and shuffling feet merging with his dreams.

He awoke to the sound of grumbling. Those of the tribe who had been sleeping around the fire were reluctantly facing a new day and the hunger and hangovers that went with it. Everyone was finding fault with everyone else, so naturally Aktuk thought it best to keep quiet. As the Small People lived very much for the day, there was nothing in the larder, and although the young men of the tribe were out hunting, there was no telling if they'd be successful or how long it would take them. So the spinsters and old men, with nothing else but time on their hands, were very snappy and cantankerous indeed. It was fortunate for Aktuk, who until recently had led such a sheltered life, that he could not understand their language; for blood-curdling oaths were being flung about in every direction. A fight broke out between two housewives, who flew at each other shrieking and sobbing, and began rolling over and over in the dust, one holding the other's hair in a painful grip, and the other with a grip on the first one's throat. Two women peacemakers threw a large deerskin over the amateur wrestlers, and held it down until lack of air forced them into a calmer state of mind. Having recovered, they both began cursing at the peacemakers, no doubt reflecting that if that's how they made peace, how would they make war? All these events greatly pleased the old men, who were cackling away in a most satisfied fashion.

Disconcerted, Aktuk began groping around for skins to sew. Several tribesmen looked at him with suspicion. To Aktuk's dismay, he'd used up all the thread, and was at a loss for what to do to appear busy and stay unnoticed. Uneasily, he caught an old man's eye. The old man spat, and shouted coarsely at him, asking why he didn't go back to his own country. Aktuk couldn't understand this, of course, but the man signalled him to leave the way he came in. Three rungs up the ladder, however, another man, outraged at seeing the slave escaping, pulled him down and flung him breathless to the ground. Miserably, Aktuk crept into a corner, and sat there hugging his knees and thinking about food.

An age later, a yell from above put an instant end to the grumbling, and everyone scrambled up the ladder. Aktuk stayed where he was, until a woman poked her head in and called to him in quite a friendly voice. Up on ground level, he found everyone gathered round two huge dead wild boars, the hunters looking modest and the others excited. The children kept putting their hands in the boars' mouths, and pulling them out with delighted shrieks. Aktuk was motioned to help with the skinning. No rituals were observed, they just hacked. Being very self-important people, they paid the Almighty the minimum of attention, and even then it was as if they were doing Him a favour. Anyway, the boars were roughly divided on the spot, some meat cut out and removed for cooking, and other juicier portions eaten raw in great handfuls. Men lunged their arms deep into the beasts' intestines, in practised search for a tasty morsel. Aktuk, though more fastidious than these hardy mortals, nevertheless managed to eat his fill. A great change came over the community, a change heralded by contented burps. The tribal mood had switched from cloudy into a long sunny period. Everyone smiled, husbands and wives again became affectionate, and even brothers and sisters once more spoke to each other. Five different people patted Aktuk on the back, as if to say, " Cheer up, youngster. " Children merrily chased each other round the trees, and adults basked in the sun, gazing fondly at their full bellies. The hunters who had captured Aktuk gazed at him with pride and approval, much as modern hunters might eye a rare beast of their capture in the zoo. Aktuk himself leant against a tree, and pondered his strange situation and the strange people he was among.

For these people were the first largely secular community he had met. In the society he had left, every act of enjoyment, from eating to sex, was held in a religious context. Yet these Small People played and danced when the mood took them, sheerly for personal amusement, and no divine retribution followed. Hadn't he left his own tribe partly because he agreed with them? And yet he could see that their cultural life was far less advanced than that of his own tribe. Kimmak had taught him that he was only here by the grace of God, and that his every action should be that of a grateful servant. Should his gratitude falter, and his servitude slacken off, he would be accused of failing the community. God is the Giver of Meat, Kimmak would say, and He only gives to those who can show their appreciation. Every member of Aktuk's tribe possessed a sense of responsibility in some measure. This was a burden, but was the Small People's way better? In his own tribe, you didn't need to squabble for choice cuts or run out to grab whatever food was available. Food would be brought to you. True, the Small People were very happy, but never for very long—next minute they'd be fighting or cursing. In his own tribe, every form of enjoyment had its own rules, and each day had a time-table, even if a very free and easy one in times of good hunting. The Small People could do as they pleased, and as a result often went hungry. Which way was best?

Two more days passed, in which Aktuk's attentions were held, forcibly, to scraping clean the hides of the two benighted wild boars. By the second day, everyone in the tribe was hungry again. To cheer themselves up, they all began to hit the heather wine, a large supply of which had just been brewed. This time Aktuk had more than a few swallows, and was pulled into the revelry by a giggling group of girls. Their hopes of being seduced proving unfounded, they consoled themselves by dressing him up in colourful beads, and daubing clay on him. Pleased with all this fuss being made of him, Aktuk sat there with a silly grin, as each new girlish idea was greeted with convulsions of laughter from the others. They all had some more wine, and the giggles blended into yawns, and Aktuk's silly grin grew sillier, until the whole party fell into an innocent, if inebriated, sleep.

The pleasant situation of awakening to find yourself on a bear skin, surrounded by beautiful semi-nude teenage girls, was somewhat wasted on Aktuk next day, for he was still unaware of some of the more basic facts of life. Nevertheless, he felt and looked absurdly contented. Before the memory of the past few days had collected itself in his early morning brain, a strange cry from above sent all the girls scrambling up the ladder. Aktuk stretched himself, and leisurely followed them. As the sun rose, a peculiar ceremony was taking place. Some young hunters had scratched a rough picture of a bison on the ground, and now stood over it menacingly, with poised spears. Through the tops of the surrounding fir trees, brilliant yellow sunlight appeared. In unison, the girls gave voice in a high, fervent and haunting chant, and the boys hurled their spears violently into the ground, all over the poor picture of a bison. Aktuk felt as embarrassed as any tourist witnessing the rituals of an alien sect. Then he thought that if hunting by pictures was so widespread, the capture of souls in drawings must be a literal fact, and what ever had he done to Alianak? He must get back to his own tribe, to set his mind at rest. Looking round, he saw that most of the older tribe members who had drunk the most, were still in bed. Unobtrusively he wandered off into the woods, and then kept wandering, glancing fearfully over his shoulder every few moments.

Two hours of wandering found him nicely lost, and at that point he would have been overjoyed to have been again captured by the Small People. Instead he found his way barred by a long stretch of thick brambles. Looking for a way round this, he found a well worn path through the middle. So he followed it, despite his discovery of hot dung and hoof prints, that showed it to be made by bison. Later, a twig snapped behind him, and turning, he beheld a huge bison bull, its tangled forehead hair giving it a quizzical look, standing some yards behind him, afraid to pass. It snuffed noisily, rolled bloodshot eyes, stamped and swished its tail. These symptoms of impatience convinced Aktuk his best place to be was in a tree. He jumped over some briars onto a low spreading branch, climbed up a little higher and waited. Soon the bison trotted by, peering short-sightedly to right and left. As its huge bulk passed Aktuk, he noticed with excitement a large jagged mark on its flanks, where members of his tribe had once hurled spears somewhat recklessly. This identified the bison as a beast familiar in Aktuk's home district—a lone bull who somehow could never be brought down by spear or arrow. When pursued, it made for the forbidden territory through which Aktuk was now trespassing. Every other day, it came down to the river to drink and wallow, and now Aktuk had stumbled on its path, a path that would lead him to within easy reach of home! After allowing his bovine benefactor a twenty minute start, Aktuk went gladly on his way.

Among Aktuk's people, some interesting developments had occurred. A search had taken place for the missing boy, but it was decidedly half-hearted, for nobody knew what to do with him if they found him. At first it was assumed that someone in the community was sheltering him, which led to accusation and counter accusation. The last straw was when Alianak's husband, out hunting in a distrait state of mind, fell into a disguised pit trap for wild pigs, of his own construction, and was killed instantly. Alianak, hitherto unruffled by the controversy ("men's foolishness" she had called it) was now inconsolable—at first she ran round and round the clearing howling her eyes out, until eventually her parents persuaded her to come home with them. Now she did no work, but just sat sadly around the house staring into space. All these troubles in the tribe came to rest on Kimmak's door-step, or cave entrance, to be more precise.

Poor Kimmak! He was now being daily pestered by earnest and aggressive young men on points of dogma about which he really cared very little. The tribe's young men, however, took ritual very seriously. Naturally their hunting skill was beyond reproach, so if an arrow missed its mark, Kimmak had to rack his brains to find a reason that would satisfy them. Not that Kimmak had lost his faith, far from it. Unlike the young men, who still gloried in the arrogance of their youth, he took nothing for granted and felt grateful each day for the privilege of being alive. His unspoken complaint against the young men was that when hunting was bad, God was blamed for taking umbrage at some unknown person's neglect of ritual. However, when hunting was good, they, the young men, took all the credit. This upset Kimmak, who made a point of calling on each hunter, to invite him to the sacred cave for a thanksgiving ceremony. As the young men's hunting ability supported the tribe, they had to be handled very carefully. No one could decide if the young men ruled Kimmak, or if Kimmak ruled the young men. Poor Kimmak was very afraid of losing his power—whenever this happened in a tribe, the result was war. The trouble was not the young men losing their faith, but rather the opposite. If anything went wrong, they would become filled with unGodly religious zeal and demand the extermination of any nearby tribe whom they blamed for offending God.

Kimmak and the young men had opposite ideas of what their religion was all about, and Kimmak had to hide this from them. If they had suspected, for example, that he regarded Life as a divine mystery, they would have demanded a more knowledgeable replacement for Shaman. To Kimmak, the works of God inspired awe, but to most of the young men, they inspired only a desire for a complete explanation. The traditional stories Kimmak told them, of God digging the sea bed with His bare hands in a single afternoon, and so on, were to him far less fantastic than the germinating seed the young men stepped unseeingly upon, or the new-born baby whose crying they complained about. Aktuk's huge pleasure in creating spontaneous elk and bison on a cave wall, struck him as something in the same line as the last two. He had high hopes of the boy as his successor, for he longed for retirement. For one thing, his periodic enslavement by the bison-spirit was very tedious, and he longed for the rest in which to meditate, and to consider ideas to expound at the Shamans' Councils. As it was, he now dreaded the next Council. He might be blamed for Aktuk's heresy, and publicly disgraced. Also, there was no one to nominate for future Shaman. The good-natured young men were not intelligent enough, and the intelligent young men were decidedly not good-natured enough. In fact, they were giving Kimmak a good deal of bother, as after the unfortunate death of Alianak's husband, they had come to him in a deputation. Did he not think that Aktuk had put a spell on the man? Kimmak doubted it. Had not Aktuk's strange behaviour somehow started a trend of bad luck? Kimmak admitted it was possible. Was it not then obvious, they pursued, that some other tribe, the Bear Tribe perhaps, was purposefully neglecting some important rites, so as to cause the wrath of God to descend on them all, via Aktuk? Kimmak for a moment wondered whether to blame the Bear Tribe, but the sound of a spear being sharpened brought home to him the consequences of that act. Hastily, he blamed everything on Keeli, the evil spirit, whose existence he did not seriously believe in for a moment. Thoughtfully, the young men walked away, and thoughtfully Kimmak watched them go. A little later, one of them came back and asked what Keeli looked like, and Kimmak pretended to be asleep.

As he lay there, he thought of the last major religious dispute, some few hundred years ago, that had passed into the annals of Shaman lore. This had centred around the discovery of artificial or man-made fire. Hitherto, fire had come direct from God during violent thunderstorms, and had then to be seized and carried into a cave on a stick, and carefully kept alive. When man-made fire, by friction, became the rule, the Shamanry declared it blasphemous and heretical. But so many people defied this rule, that they were forced to reconsider. If a blessing was uttered at the moment the sparks flew, all would be well. This wise move ended the fire raising craze, which destroyed many woods, people and animals, because the blessing was so long and complicated that henceforth up to the present day, no one lit a fire unless it was absolutely necessary. Had the time come, Kimmak wondered, to declare all art free from the bonds of religion, even as fire was freed? He had seen, and marvelled, that Alianak's picture had no obvious and direct connection with her soul. Perhaps human beings, having stronger individuality than other animals, were not bound by the laws applied by God to the rest of His creation—at this point, Kimmak did really fall asleep.

As Kimmak slept, four young men gathered in secret to discuss Keeli. If Keeli was so powerful, they reasoned, was it not worth their while to defect to him? The boldest of the company drew Keeli on the ground, with a sharp stick, while the others stood by, ready to run if anything happened. Many miles away, in the Alps, lived the ill famed Ibex Tribe, famous for its sexual perversions. Stories of these inspired the young man to portray Keeli as a form of Ibex Spirit, or human goat. Admiringly, the others looked on. The bold young man knelt to Keeli and appeared to pray, while his companions shuffled their feet uneasily, keeping a weather eye out for thunderbolts. At length, the young man spoke.

" I will tell you the message Keeli has revealed to me !

If we worship him, instead of God, he will grant us these freedoms. Any girl we like, married or unmarried, we can take, providing we draw her picture first!"

At first this revelation was distinctly popular, but then one timid soul enquired if the husbands and boyfriends would understand about Keeli.

"That brings me to the second freedom!" went on the Chosen One pompously. "Providing we draw their picture first, we can safely kill any one of the husbands or boyfriends."

No one wanted to seem so naïve as to disapprove of this, but the timid soul wanted to know what Kimmak would say and do.

"Kimmak is powerless, because he is a Man of God, and Keeli has power over God," was the reply. Another boy asked whether Aktuk was therefore a villain or a hero. Before the Chosen One had time to think of Keeli's reply, an outsider burst shouting into their midst.

"To spears, everyone! Old Scar-Shanks, the unbeatable bison, has waded far down the river! We need many men to prevent him from returning to the forbidden forest! Glory to the one who can bring him down! Come on, come on!"

Thus the creation of a class of dissenting intellectuals was temporarily postponed, and the hunter in each man sprang to the surface, for after all, each man was a hunter. The bison itself was old and lacking in protein, and its appeal was similar to that of an unconquered peak to a dedicated mountaineer. Vaguely, the idea was felt that with Old Scar-Shanks' death, the impossible being achieved, an era of good fortune would fall upon the tribe. No less than twenty-five hunters of all ages were hot on the trail. Their only hope would be to encircle the beast before it reached the edge of the forbidden forest, which it well knew to be its sanctuary. Once more, however, they were too late, as the bison charged madly for Tom Tiddler's Ground only a few yards ahead of their spears. Their superior numbers were of no use to them now—only one man was needed to stand in the beast's way to make it change course, but naturally no one dared enter the out-of-bounds zone, for fear of supernatural reprisal.

Then the impossible happened—with a snort, Old Scar-Shanks reappeared at the forest edge, a look of wild indecision in his rolling eyes. Before he had time to plunge in again, he had become a sad, sagging pin-cushion of spears and arrows. A full life behind him, he lay down heavily on one side, which knocked a spear towards his heart and sent him on his way to that great buffalo pasture in the sky. No one was sure who had done the most to kill the beast, but that was not what their shouted conversation was all about. No, they wanted to know whatever had caused him to come blundering out of his sanctuary again.

As if in answer, Aktuk innocently stumbled through the undergrowth at the forest's edge, grotesquely decorated with alien beads and daubs of clay. No one spoke, unless gasps of amazement are speech. Finally, one hunter, a sensible married man of thirty-five with a ferocious black beard and moustache, found his voice.

" Did you come out of the forbidden forest? " he asked.

" Well, yes—it wasn't my fault—— "

" You must have strong magic. I hope you mean to use it wisely, for your tribe. "

" Er, yes, yes, of course. "

" I hope you mean it. Certainly, sending us Old Scar-Shanks is a magnificent start. What are those beads and markings? "

" Well, the Small People gave me them. I've been staying with them. "

This caused a great sensation, for in the tribe's estimation, the Small People were unpredictable spirits. After a hasty consultation, the bearded one took Aktuk home, while the others trimmed saplings and finally made a rough sledge to drag and push their victim home on. As Aktuk tremblingly entered the settlement, he was nearly knocked down by the people's amazed stares, his mother's included. Silently, the hunter guided him to Kimmak's cave and left him there. Kimmak gave the boy some food and drink and listened very attentively to his story. After that they both talked far into the night, especially Kimmak, while the other citizens grew wakeful through wondering what the morning would bring.

Both Kimmak and Aktuk had a long lie in, finally arising after the sun was high in the sky. A deferential hunter, full of forboding, brought them a delicious breakfast, and then lingered, catching Kimmak's eye and looking away again. Everyone in the tribe felt that something of significance was about to happen. Just as the hunter was clearing his throat for an awkward goodbye, Kimmak casually told him to ask all the men to congregate in the sacred cave, at noon, which was in an hour's time. Brightening up at once, the hunter assured Kimmak four or five times that he would carry out his wishes, and then trotted back to the agog populace, swelling with pride.

Having compared notes and put their heads together, Kimmak and Atkuk had decided on some Church reforms which would benefit both them and the community. It only remained necessary to convince the people of Aktuk's good faith, and to this end, Kimmak had composed one of his rather pompous speeches, and taught it to Aktuk as best as he could in the time.

At noon, all the men gathered and sat cross legged and open mouthed. The Keeli conspirators glanced furtively at each other, wondering if they were due to be denounced. First, Kimmak spoke :—

"People of the Tribe, I call on you to open your hearts in welcome to someone you all know, who has been away from us, not, as some good but mistaken people have claimed, for any evil purpose, but solely for reasons of garnering wisdom and God-inspired knowledge. This knowledge will soon be available to us all, for I am shortly going to call upon Aktuk to speak to you. " (Those of the tribe who had seen Aktuk run out of the same cave, not to seek God, but in fear of his life, marvelled at the faultiness of their memory.) " But before Aktuk speaks, (Kimmak continued) it is my duty to clear him of a very serious charge. Our beloved brother who so recently and prematurely joined his ancestors, was not in any way the victim of spells or enchantment. I, and I am sure I speak for all of you, am very well aware that Aktuk has not even a spark of malice in his soul, and was indeed as shocked as any of you when I acquainted him with the tragic story . . . "

Aktuk's feelings on hearing of the passing of Alianak's

husband had actually been somewhat mixed. Anyhow, Kimmak, well warmed up, was about to enlarge in greater detail on Aktuk's soul and its unrivalled purity, but sensing the crowd's impatience, he stepped aside and allowed Aktuk the foreground.

"People of the Tribe," the youthful prophet began, and then halted.

"Go on!" Kimmak urged, in a stage whisper.

"Well, People of the Tribe, you are well aware of the pleasures of life granted to us by the Almighty God, the Giver of Meat."

"Eating!" cried one hungry soul who had missed his breakfast.

"Eating, yes," said Aktuk with a benevolent smile—he was getting the hang of things. Never was a first sermon more important. "But my friends, we are people, and I refer to the pleasures of life God has granted us alone, of all the living creatures; painting, dancing and music—this is what I mean. Because all of these reflect the glory of God, you, who are hunters, cannot enjoy them to the extent the Shamanry can. But during my time in the forbidden forest, God took care of me, and guided my feet to the homes of the Small People. There I learnt this great truth, that any man may sing or dance or draw without angering God, as some of you have witnessed on the day I drew Alianak. A song or a dance need not be sacred, it can be on any topic. A man is not an elk, for his soul to be easily captured. God has strengthened man's soul, and anything a man does that brings innocent pleasure to himself and to others, is glorifying God whether His name be directly mentioned or not."

A buzz of conversation arose, as people excitedly pictured in their minds the great things they would do. A minority, however, looked afraid, as if the world were about to end. Meanwhile, Aktuk continued :—

" Without any doubt at all, I assure you that if you wish to draw the portraits of your loved ones, you may do so, not in the face of divine vengeance, but in the certainty of divine blessing. " (This last phrase was pure Kimmak.)

Everyone became restless, filled with the urge to run home and paint portraits of their wives and children. The excitement was tremendous.

" Long live Aktuk! " someone shouted, and others took up the cry, including the boy who had chosen himself in Keeli's name. Seeing this, the others in his group forgot all about Keeli, with a great sense of relief. Of course Keeli was not yet dead—for he can be said to live, in the backs of men's minds—and he would manifest himself many a time more in the course of human history.

Kimmak again took the floor.

" Before you go, my people, I trust I may speak for Aktuk at the forthcoming Council—it *is* your wish he become the next Shaman? "

" Aktuk for ever! He who conquered Scar-Shanks is a worthy leader! " shouted another individual, amid murmurs of assent.

So it was that Aktuk became groomed in every detail of the Shamanry, just as if nothing had happened. Only now he had a fanatical following, that, as time went by, would subside into the love and loyalty that Kimmak enjoyed. Atkuk's helplessness was also a good asset—it pleased the people that their leader, for all his powers, was utterly dependent on them to keep alive; and men and women alike went out of their way to do him favours. Kimmak eventually retired, happy in the certainty that he had done his duty by both Tribe and God. For with the new wave of interest in the arts, the young men's thoughts of war and dogma became far more sketchy and infrequent. As often seems to happen in the world of ideas, the notion of "Art for Pleasure's Sake" had been spontaneously engendered in heads in many different and widely separated parts of the country, and Shamans who opposed it fought a losing battle. However, the average hunter, being a man of technical ability, preferred to carve faces on bone and stone to painting, which still had ecclesiastical overtones. Hence the many beautifully sculptured women's heads in jade and in various stones, that are still being unearthed in the district today. A sense came to all the tribes, that they, of all God's creatures, had a big part to play in Destiny. This ancient, unrecorded Renaissance stimulated human progress as never before, and all over the world, for the next few hundred years, the wheel was being individually invented animals were being tamed, and experimental drawings were made that would lead to literature. Religion and Art, from being one, became as a man and wife, sometimes on good terms with each other, sometimes not so good. Naturally, this new thought, and the increase in property, led to bitter quarrels and loss of life, but this could not kill the optimistic spirit of the times.

At the time, Kimmak sometimes mentally reproached himself for slightly falsifying Aktuk's story for the common good. But during his ensuing years of meditation, he concluded that Aktuk's genius for lucky accident and coincidence must have been God-given. He was being continually surprised by the huge potentialities of the human spirit, and as idea followed idea, it seemed as if God was pouring more and more of Himself into the human race, to the possible detriment of the rest of creation.

Of course, most of this artistic ability was among the men. The women of Aktuk's tribe had long been hardened eye-rollers. By this I mean that they were long used to their husbands babbling on about politics, religion, magic and warfare, and only rolled their eyes up to Heaven to witness how much a good woman must endure; before continuing to cook, clean, sew and rear children, as they had always done and always will do. All of which activity, of course, the men, being men, took entirely for granted, and providing it was all done exactly to their convenience, they indeed only vaguely noticed it was going on.

The first sculptured figure presented to a preoccupied wife by her excited husband was greeted with the weary question, "Can you eat it?" This piece of feminine sarcasm resulted in the wife getting a clip round the ear and the husband stalking out to ferociously attack an innocent reindeer that happened to be wandering about. Later however, when her work was done, the woman looked at her portrait in stone, and considered the thought behind it, and concluded that for a piece of men's foolishness, it was remarkably good. She tidied up the cave and asked her neighbours on each side in to see it. They clucked and oohed over it, and then recollected that *their* husbands were spending their spare time on something very similar. For the first time, the wives didn't need to merely humour their husbands, but could actually work up an interest in their ridiculous activities.

As for Alianak, Kimmak thought it only decent to let an interlude of time pass, before doing a little match-making on Aktuk's behalf. So six days after Aktuk's return, Kimmak chose accidentally to meet Alianak as she gathered water at the river. They talked together quietly for a long time. Alianak certainly needed a husband, for she was already with child.

" When's he due for the manhood initiation? " she asked.

" Next week, with the other young boys. "

" Kimmak? " She leaned over him confidentially.

" Yes, " he answered.

" Teach him all you know, " she entreated earnestly.

Minutes later, Aktuk almost flew to Alianak's side. His sojourn in the wilderness, brief though it had been, had given him a look of confidence that surprised and delighted Alianak, who in turn shot him such a look of affection that a thrill of love shook his whole being; and soon the conversation led around to weddings, the superiority of short engagements and to the patter of little feet.

" You sure you don't mind our first being—well, being, um, more mine than yours? " Alianak asked, her head on his shoulder, her eyes closed.

" Of course not. I'll be a perfect father, you wait and see. His real father, now, you must admit, was a rough and ready person. Look how coarsely he treated you . . . "

"Ah, shut up!" cried Alianak, as this had brought back memories too nostalgic to be endured. Side by side they sat, watching the waters of the river slipping past them, forgetting their troubles and certainly forgetting the clay pot intended to be filled for Alianak's mother. This utterly nondescript clay pot fell into the river, was swept along a little way, and then stuck in a bed of mud. Aktuk and Alianak are now forgotten, as are all the people of the Bison Tribe, but the clay pot, somewhat the worse for wear, stands in a place of honour in a well-known museum. Pamphlets have been written about it, and it has caused reputations to be made and lost.